THROUGH HER EYES

One Family's Journey
From Enslavement
To The Great Migration

Arthur Vaughn

Foreword By Rosa Mae Derricott

Library of Congress Cataloging – in- Publication Data has been applied for.

Paperback ISBN: 979-8-9885806-0-7

PRINTED IN THE UNITED STATES OF AMERICA.

Book Publishing Services by Pen Legacy LLC. (www.penlegacy.com)

FIRST EDITION

Table of Contents

A Letter from Rosa Mae

1459 Union St
Bklyn N.Y. 11213
March 25, 1998

Dear Arthur:-

Received your letter of recent date and can
Was er very glad to hear from you. The plans
for a family reunion are great. Hopefully
every one will plan and be there. It is get/in
late for some of us and I am referring to myself.
My health seems to be fairly well and I go
as often as possible. Was at Adrian's home
for my birthday. Had a nice time. Was not
as active as I ought to have been but I
liked being there and meeting some of
her friends. There was also to be a party
at my church for me but I suppose
they decided that the one party was
enough. They did not give me any
excuse nor apology. The pastor's birthday
was the 15th and I heard nothing about it.
But I believe they did give him a donation
which is better than a party in my
opinion.

About the reunion am sending the re—
quired amount asked for if Tibley did not
send it. I assume that her and I are one
house hold. David is not at home. He is

Dedication

When I set out to write this book, I wanted to document the stories my grandmother shared with me during our many conversations and her written words. Through my research, I got so much more out of this than I ever expected. During a pilgrimage to Union County, South Carolina, I stood on the same ground my previously enslaved ancestors had walked. I visited the gravesites of my enslaved ancestors and the gravesite of the enslaver, our earliest known ancestor in the United States.

My grandmother, Rosa Mae Woodall, is the inspiration for this series of short stories. Grandma—or Ma to some of my cousins—set the stage for all of us. I miss the Sunday dinners at her home on Union Street in Brooklyn and her famous dinner rolls. Each family has a legacy, and with the writing of this book, it is my prayer that our legacy is not forgotten but is told for generations to come.

Arthur Vaughn, Ed.D.

Foreword

*You are not judged by the height you have risen but from the
depth you have climbed.*

– Frederick Douglas

In a dimly lit room, pains from miscarriage rang out, and
children gathered around their mother's bed. Pop couldn't
quite decide what to do. The children wouldn't leave their
mother's side, and Momma was sweating profusely while
looking to her husband and Aunt Sallie for guidance. Should
they go to the hospital where the white folks were liable to
kill them, or should they stay home and pray God's will be
done?

Aunt Sallie told Pop, "I don't want my sister to go to the
slaughterhouse pen."

"Ahhh!"

Another cry rang out as the pain shot through Momma's
body.

"Rosa Mae, get the children out of here!" Pop ordered.

It wouldn't be until after midnight that they realized

Arthur Vaughn

Mama's quietness was not a sign she had gotten better. Her asking to go to sleep and for Pop to mind the knee baby was not a good sign. Rosa Mae and Pop would hear Mama gasp her last breath as she went into eternity.

Rosa Mae Hill was born in 1911 and was around twelve years of age when her mother passed. She didn't know her mother wouldn't make it. She hadn't expected to become a surrogate mother at her age. She didn't know how to raise children and take care of a home. A part of Rosa Mae changed that day. Her life altered, and as she says, her childhood was over.

In his book, *Through Her Eyes*, Dr. Arthur Vaughn pays homage to Rosa Mae Hill, our grandmother. Rosa Mae Hill was the matriarch of our family and left a legacy of hard work, perseverance, and faith in God. Dr. Vaughn is one of countless others who are her legacy in action. It is with great honor that I, his first cousin, have gotten to see this legacy exuded in him. His volunteer work for the American Heart Association, 100 Black Men of America, and serving as chair for several community organizations in the Atlanta metro area is an effort to give others what has been given to him in principle and deed.

Dr. Vaughn has worked as a senior administrator in higher education and served as executive director at Morehouse School of Medicine, where he provided academic and research financial support. Dr. Vaughn is also a heart transplant survivor, which has shaped his life in different ways since 2019. He has used this time post-transplant to reflect on his life and the life of his ancestors.

Dr. Vaughn's work is near to me. In addition to being the great-granddaughter of Ella Lloyd and Benjamin Franklin

Hill, I am Rosa Mae Hill's granddaughter and Dr. Arthur Vaughn's first cousin. My research in decolonizing education helps me to frame this work in the continuum of struggle and freedom. Our great-grandparents left South Carolina in search of a better life in Philadelphia and ultimately settled in Brooklyn, New York. I wonder if they envisioned the life we have now. Not only would their children move forward in life, but their great-grandchildren would continue the climb up from slavery. Rosa Mae Hill recorded portions of her life in letters to the family. We hope all readers can find strength in these letters and hope in the unseen.

Rosa Mae Derricott, Ed.D

Introduction

I take the baton from my ancestors so one day I can pass it to our descendants.

– Hank Stewart

Benjamin Franklin Hill, who we called Pop, would sit around the pot belly stove with us and share a thousand stories about his mother, Phoebe Dawkins, our first ancestor who knew freedom. Grandma Phoebe—born in 1860 and having the features of a mixed-race woman—was raised on the plantation where her father, Randle, and his mother, Katy, were once enslaved. Our family history was important to Pop. He wanted the family to understand what life was like for the Black folk that came before us. He wanted to ensure our legacy was passed down through the stories and legends he would tell after Sunday dinner.

Pop would tell us how Grandma Phoebe would be at her grandmother Katy's feet while she made her famous rolls on

Massa Dawkins' plantation. He would share with us how the enslaved would use scraps left from slaughtered animals, boiled grains, and a creative mixture of fruits, vegetables, and other items to sustain themselves. Through ingenuity, they took what was given to them and created the foundations of what became known as soul food.

The South Carolina plantation of enslaver William "Bill" McKinley Dawkins is where the earliest recollection of our family history is known. I'm Benjamin Franklin Hill's firstborn child, Rosa Mae, and this is our story.

Architecture of The Dawkins' Plantation

Going to Meet the Man

As dawn broke and the sun peaked through the early morning sky, the tree-lined canopy along the quarter-mile red clay path to the great house gradually came into view. A six-foot-three lanky in stature Bill Dawkins stepped out on the upper deck of his antebellum-era mansion. Dawkins, a fifth-generation American of Scots–Irish descent, was born on August 1, 1790, and was the eldest and wealthiest of the six brothers and two sisters born to Thomas Dawkins (1764–1839) and Sarah Oester (1763–1849). Bill and his brothers made their futures through farming and participating in the slave trade in the 1800s. Dew dripped from the cotton rose bushes that adorned the fountain in the center of the horseshoe entryway leading up to the four-pillar, two-story home. As was common, Dawkins'

Replica of the Dawkins Family Plantation located in Union County, South Carolina. (A.D. Vaughn Collection)

monotone voice called out for Tom Meeks, the massa's voice cutting through the quiet morning fog.

"Meeks!"

Dawkins waited a moment before calling out for Meeks once more.

"Meeks!"

Out of the shadows, an imposing figure replied, "How can I help you, boss?"

Tom Meeks was also a Scottish immigrant, hired to oversee the roughly 1,300-acre plantation Massa Dawkins purchased from A.W. Thompson in 1825 in Union County, South Carolina. Meeks was a failed sharecropper indebted to Massa Dawkins and forced to work to pay off what he owed. He made his way by training others on how to break slaves and manage smaller plantations. Meeks' ill temperament and willingness to inflict pain made him well-suited to run a plantation. Meeks was a white man, but he recognized his place as subordinate to the plantation owner and never failed to call Bill Dawkins either Boss or Mr. Dawkins. The two men were not peers, and their differing stations in life were clear. However, Meeks was still a white man and, as such, was afforded a higher status than the American Indian or the Colored. Meeks—a man of few words and who had a reputation of being harsh and demanding to the field hands and holding little regard for the enslaved that worked in the planter's residence.

Massa Dawkins could stand on the grand balcony, then look right and left as far as the eye could see and know all that land was his. The Dawkins' plantation was in what was known as Upstate South Carolina and sat on Bowles Hill. It was one of the largest in the area, providing corn, cattle, and cotton to the region, the northern states, and parts of Europe.

The southern areas of South Carolina were referred to as the Lowcountry or Gold Coast. Lowcountry sits at or below sea level. The Gullah people there were prominent, clinging to aspects of their African heritage, including crafts and folktales (Olwell, 1998). The cash crop in the Lowcountry was rice, which required ten times as much slave labor than the crops grown in Upstate. The incidence of slavery was greater in the Lowcountry, as growing and cultivating rice was common in African nations. The enslaved populations in South Carolina were stolen mainly from Angola, Senegambia, and the Windward Coast (Menard, 1994; Lewis, 1985; Olwell, 1998).

Over one hundred enslaved American Indians and Africans worked on Massa Dawkins' plantation. The American Indians often ran off and were difficult to capture because they knew the land well and could find refuge within the other tribes. The Africans were much easier to identify and had fewer allies among the indigenous people (Gallay, 2009). Bill shared with Meeks that they must replace the Indians (natives) with more Africans and that he would head to Charleston and purchase a few new slaves.

"I will take Coffey with me. He does well with picking bucks and wenches, and he will make fine company during the journey."

Coffey was a Colored, but as a slave driver, he served as a fitting complement to Meeks in managing slaves.

Some of Massa Dawkins' favored slaves served as taskmasters, supporting the overseers' work, and spies that reported back any mischievous behavior of the other slaves. Drivers had the worst of both the free and enslaved worlds—one foot in both and welcomed in neither. Drivers were forced to mete out punishment to the enslaved who did not perform.

Viewed as traitors to their people, they were hated by their fellow Coloreds (VanDeburg, 1978). They were not afforded the special privileges of the overseer and were considered nothing more than a Colored for Massa's amusement and bidding. On one hand, overseer Meeks, a harsh and deliberate man, had no qualms disciplining the enslaved Indians and Africans with his rawhide whip. On the other hand, the white men saw Coffey as a joke—an old minstrel negro. In the view of the other enslaved, he was a traitor and a snake.

Massa Dawkins was a heavy-handed man who did not tolerate those who did not produce in the field, his mills, or the big house. Like many slaveholders, Dawkins would hand-select enslaved men, women, and chillun with no regard for existing relationships and force them to engage in sexual relationships intended to produce the best offspring. They were treated like cattle, and those who did not produce children as expected were punished with a firm hand and lashed across their backs with a whip (Smithers, 2012).

The crops on the Dawkins plantation were expanding and needed extra hands to keep up. Bill understood that slave labor was needed to work the land and viewed them as property no different than cattle. The enslaved were essential to his wealth. Owning such a large amount of land and property made Bill Dawkins an important man in the local community and the state. As a single man, he would have been a catch for any of the local women who often made known their availability and desire to be Bill's wife.

Drivers like Coffey and house slaves were considered higher ranking and were comparatively well off (VanDeburg, 1978). In addition to fieldwork, the enslaved might become artisans in the mills, blacksmiths, or learn to make bricks. Of all the enslaved, craftsmen were the best off. They were neither treated like domesticated pets like the house Coloreds nor abused like plantation cattle, as were the field Coloreds. The house Coloreds were controlled by the constant threat of being demoted to a common field worker, whose lives were significantly harsher (Harper, 1978).

Coffey recalled punishment being handed out during a festive occasion for other white plantation owners and their friends. The other enslaved often witnessed retributions as a deterrent to remain in line or not run off. These horrifying exhibits left many of the enslaved emotionally broken. When a man is hunted like a wild beast, he forgets there is a God in heaven. He forgets everything beyond the reach of the slave catcher.

Later the same morning, Coffey loaded the horse-drawn wagon, and he and Bill started on the 176-mile journey to Charleston, leaving Meeks to run the plantation. During the 16-hour trip, Coffey amused his master with songs and tales of the activities around the plantation. Bill laughed the entire way to Charleston but dreaded the return trip. If he purchased more slaves than would fit in the carriage, the return trip would take 2.5 days with the slaves walking behind the carriage. If he purchased American-born slaves, they were usually broken in and easier to transport, whereas the Africans who recently arrived in this country were unruly and would often attempt to escape during transport back to the plantation. The challenges related to purchasing unbroken slaves weighed heavily on Dawkins' mind during the trip.

Upon arriving in Charleston, Bill visited the home of Nathaniel and Sarah Russell. Russell made his fortune in the mercantile business, selling many of the goods Bill produced on his plantation (Zierden, 1999). The local hotels were packed on account of the large slave auction scheduled for the next day. However, Dawkins was not concerned because, as was common, he stayed at the Russell's home.

The Nathaniel Russell House was built in 1808 by wealthy merchant and slave trader, Nathaniel Russell. It is recognized as one of America's most important neo-classical houses. (Courtesy of The Library of Congress).

Bill stepped outside and directed Coffey to take the wagon down to the stable, clean up the horses, and bed them down for the night. Being an enslaved Colored in the South, Coffey could not just move freely in Charleston, so Dawkins made sure he had papers saying Coffey was his property. If he were stopped, Coffey would present his ownership papers to any white man who questioned him and tell them, "Sir, I am Massa Dawkins' Colored. He told me to bring these horses to the stable, clean 'em, and get 'em fed."

Edward Rainey

After the horses were taken care of, Coffey returned to the back of the stable to join the other slave drivers who accompanied their masters to the auction. As he was ready to shut his eyes, he heard an odd voice call out.

"Can someone please help me with my horse and wagon?"

Not used to hearing someone say please, he jumped up to see who the strange voice belonged to. A man—tall enough that Coffey had to look up to him—stood there dressed in the finest clothes Coffey ever saw on a Colored man.

"Sir, how may I help you?"

"I will pay you five cents to feed and put my horse and buggy away for me."

Coffey jumped at the opportunity to get paid for work he had done for free all his life.

As the man began to walk away, Coffey asked, "Mister, who is you?"

"I am Edward Rainey. I run the barbershop down the street."

Coffey's mouth fell open, and his eyes showed disbelief. Coffey had never seen a Colored man who was allowed to work for himself. A Colored who dressed like a white man and was paid for his work. Imagine that!

Even though Rainey was a Colored, when Coffey told this story to the other enslaved men who had traveled with their enslavers to the auction, he referred to Edward Rainey as Massa Rainey. Massa was the only way he knew to refer to men of power and distinction. He shared with the others the way Rainey spoke and how he walked the streets without local white men stopping him for his freedom papers. Years later, Edward and Gracie Rainey's son, Joseph H. Rainey, would become the first African American to serve in the United States House of Representatives (Amer, 2005).

Hon. Joseph H. Rainey,
South Carolina, ca. 1865.
(Courtesy National Archives)

Weeping Time

Coffey and the other enslaved who traveled with their masters stayed in the stables with the horses overnight. Dawkins and other plantation owners were not overly concerned about the slaves running off because the drivers were like the house Coloreds; they loved their masters more than the masters loved themselves. The driver and the house Colored would give their life to save their master's house. If the master's house caught on fire, the house Colored would fight harder to put the blaze out than the master. If the master got sick, the house Colored would ask, "What's the matter, Massa? We sick?" He identified himself with his master more than his master identified with himself (Benton, 2016).

Coffey made sure not to leave the stable as he might be beaten by any white man on the street or mistaken for a runaway and shot or hung. Coffey knew what could happen if he was found on the street unaccompanied at night. So, he made sure he stayed where he belonged and did what he was told. As he lay on the pile of hay that he managed to fashion into a bed, he could hear the slaves moanin' and prayin' and frettin' about what was to come in the mornin'!

The following day, a sign was posted proclaiming there was to be a public sale of Coloreds, horses, and chattel. Massa Dawkins and Coffey headed to the open area north of the Old Exchange Building at Broad and East Bay Streets for the weekly slave auction.

Old Exchange Building in Charleston, South Carolina.
(Courtesy Low Country Digital Library)

The Olde Exchange Building is an important piece of American History. During the Revolutionary War, the British used the bottom level of this building as a prison where those seen as enemies to the crown were held. Later, this building was where the state's political leaders debated and then ratified the United States Constitution (McInnis, 2005).

Charleston was all abuzz with the visitors speculating on the prices of the human merchandise that would be on exhibition. Starting in the 16th century and ending in the 19th century, 12.5 million enslaved Africans were stolen from their tribes, with 11 million making it to American shores. About forty percent of enslaved Africans brought into the country passed through Charleston Harbor (Higgins, 1976).

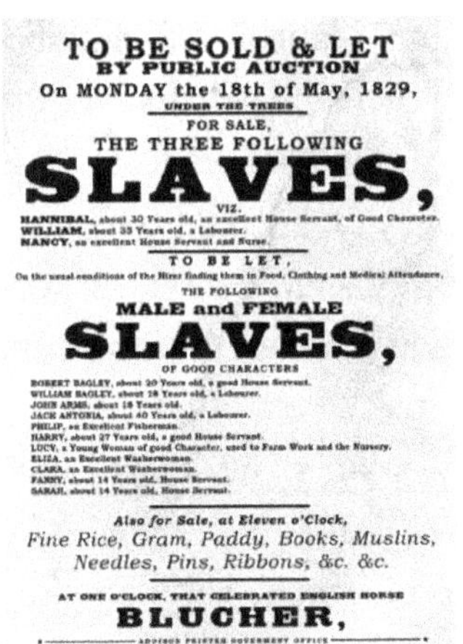

This day's auction was a result of three Virginia plantations falling on hard times that led to the need to sell off property. Most of the slaves grew up on the plantations and had never been sold before. On many southern plantations, the value attached to the enslaved surpassed that of the homes and land. There were instances that were rarely discussed, but some of the enslaved being sold was rumored to be the chillun of their massas.

One of the largest slave auctions held in South Carolina was set to take place. One hundred and twenty-three prime

Coloreds—men, women, chillun, and infants—were to be put up for auction. Slave masters and their representatives from North and South Carolina, Georgia, Alabama, and Louisiana were in attendance for this massive event.

"Dere lots of white folks dere come to look over all these Coloreds at dis auction," Coffey was heard to say.

Coffey would tell stories of how the massas would look over the enslaved to consider their value. The enslaved men, women, and chillun would be stripped to the waist and led out on a platform for examination. The seller would slather his slaves with oil to disguise blemishes on their skin and make them look healthier. In certain instances, the women and men were displayed stark naked to see the extent of blemishes on their bodies. Those scarred or welted were considered less valuable and sold at a lower cost than those without marks. The potential buyers pulled open the enslaved mouths to gawk at their teeth, forced them to walk around to detect any signs of lameness, and pinched their limbs to determine muscularity. It was humiliating. The cruelty inherent in one human being's ability to own and sell another to the highest bidder was on full display this day. Slaves from 18–30 years of age brought in the most money (Johnson, 2009).

We were not sure how much of Coffey's tales were true, or if he was just trying to scare us so we didn't get any funny ideas about running away from Massa Dawkins.

"Dere am tears comin' down the woman's cheeks as I put dem in irons and led them to the wagon," Coffey recounted.

Auctions always bothered Coffey as he watched chillun torn away from their mammies and pappies and sold off. He remembered when he was sold off from his old mammy, whom he never saw again. He had been sold to Massa Dawkins when he was just a little boy and did not remember his first massa's name.

The auction block was a horrific scene where mothers and fathers were sold and parted from their chillun. Others fought not to be sold, crying out, "Lord! Lord!" while kicking and screaming as they were dragged away (McInnis, 2011).

The enslaved at this auction were sold in droves like cattle, which they called ruffigees. It was hard to believe the Lord would let people live who were so harsh.

In the distance,

Katy could hear the auctioneer singing the praises of his merchandise.

"Gentlemen, here is a big, black buck Colored. Good for any kin' o' work, an' he never gives no problems. He will work like your best mule. We are selling this Colored to the highest bidder."

"Den dere am three or four other Coloreds sold befo' Massa Dawkins began bidding," said Coffey.

"'We have some young Colored wenches for sale today," the auctioneer said. "They'll be good for house or field work and are ready to breed."

Two other men am biddin' on the gals, but Massa back dem down and won the bid. Coffey heard the Colored traders say, "The woman had never been 'bused—sexually abused, that is––and will make good for breeding." Women who hadn't been 'bused were better for breeding, had fewer issues during childbirth, and were more valuable.

Massa Dawkins purchased one mulatto woman named Katy, two other adult women—Rosetta and Milley—and Milley's young daughter, Lucy, for $1,500.25.

On the day Katy was sold to Massa Dawkins, Coffey saw seven chillun torn from their mother and led to the auction block.

Arthur Vaughn

They mama knew several would be gone from her care, but when all were sold, she wept uncontrollably, asking God to take her life (McInnis, 2011).

"I seed lots of Coloreds put on the block and bid off and carry away in chains on that day. Later that day, we starts home with these wenches in chains in the back of the wagon."

Notes of a Native Daughter:
Katy's Story

Letters of a Slave Family

I am Katy Dawkins, born into slavery in 1802 in Virginia but sold away from my family when I was five years old. Word has it I am the grandchild of one of President George Washington's kin, but there was no evidence to prove it. No white man would admit to fathering a child from a Colored woman, so I never knew who my daddy was for sure.

Upon arriving on Massa Dawkins' plantation, I saw the big house and was heard saying it looks as if it stood one hundred foot off the ground. 'Course, I did not know what one hundred foot was, but I knew the house was big.

I wondered if I was to work in the house or in the field. I never saw a woman work with dem in the ironworks or other shops, so I figured I wouldn't be working there. Several white men directed work on the plantation and a few traitorous Coloreds, like Coffey, who did anything to please them. All of us new to the plantation were set to toil in the fields, day after day.

Coffey led me to the slave quarters. My cabin was a small wooden shack with a tin roof and a dirt floor. I was to share this space with nine other enslaved females. The only space I could pretend to call my own was a wood pallet in the corner. Women that have been there longer had bunk beds with blankets to keep themselves warm on the cold nights. The first night on my narrow pallet, I moaned and wept. I felt abandoned and alone.

On Massa Dawkins' plantation, we planted sweet corn as soon as the winter frost was gone. Coffey told us it was a hard crop to grow up north and did better closer to the coast, but Mr. Meeks insisted that we worked and bring in Massa's crops.

Ya see, the really good soil for corn was close to the water, and they started planting there in March a whole month before we started. Corn would grow up in sixty to ninety days after planting, so we had to get that cotton picked quick so Massa could get his corn crop planted and to the market in time. Some of us would be planting corn, while others planted cotton. We would work until dem crops was laid. As the new gal, the overseers sent me to the cotton fields.

When the fields started sprouting, we would all make sure we tended to them and kept the weeds from taking hold. This wasn't easy work at all. We couldn't tell where Massa's land started or ended. Each day we would work from before the sun come up till after it went down to make sure the crop come in good. Chillun, as young as five, wore a harness to tote tools, buckets, or other supplies to field hands. Some chillun brought us water from time to time, but the white folks wouldn't bother wasting food on us during the workday. Little attention was paid to slaves' meals. Even the pigs and mules ate during the day, but not the enslaved.

There was a time or two when work would stop so we could tend to someone who passed out or was birthing a baby in the field, but as soon as that passed, we were back to work.

Come September, we worked together to pick the cotton

crop. I never forgot how us field hands, including the chillun, had daily measures to meet. The women were often expected to do half the work as a grown man, but don't be mistaken; the labor was tough. The planting fields were mostly tended by women, as the men were busy raising cattle and calves. Massa would hire some of us out in the winter months to other plantation owners when tending to the cotton and corn fields was slow. We soon learned who was the kind and mean massas in the area. If you were going to be hired out, ya prayed for one of the kinder plantation owners.

Ole Bessy

Over time, I began to be accepted by the other slave families. An older woman who had been with Massa for some time took me in and made me feel as "at home" as any enslaved person could. Ole Bessy looked out for me the best she could.

"Come here, child, and let me patch up dem tattered clothes," Bessy would say.

When she could, she would give me something new to wear from hand-me-downs that Massa's nieces would give her. In fact, Bessy made clothing for many of the enslaved, and I was happy to have a friend.

If God granted beauty upon a slave girl, it was the greatest curse. The same qualities that command admiration in the white woman draw hatred toward the female slave. Slavery is terrible for men but far worse for women. Every day we learned what it meant to be a slave—to be unprotected by law or custom. Slavery made the slaveholder cruel and hedonistic and his sons violent and immoral. It sullied daughters and made wives insecure (Jacobs, 2022; Renka, 2002). At the same time that we were fending off weeds and bugs, women were fending off the advances of men folk—both the slave and the white man. It was when I turned fifteen years old that Massa began whispering foul words in my ear.

For a time, Ole Bessy was able to keep Massa's focus away from me. Since I worked in the field, Massa did not see me daily, and I could often escape his torment. Ole Bessy was able to manage Mr. Meeks and the other overseers pretty good when it came to me, but other negro women were subjected to the desires of both free and enslaved men. I later learned it wasn't Ole Bessy but Massa who put the word out that I was to be busted by him and no other. Massa Dawkins threatened a reckoning on any man who violated his directive.

Massa never married, yet it was known Massa had already fathered children with two of his house negros, Milley and Rosetta. Now he was eyeing me. Massa Dawkins believed in breaking in the house wenches and fathering the firstborn of each. There were no good slaveholders, but some had concubine relationships with many of their enslaved women (Jacobs, 2022). Like many plantation owners, Massa Dawkins had sexually assaulted enslaved women and made others serve as bed warmers (Renka, 2002). I remember stories from Milley (1805–1885) and Rosetta (1805–1880) about how Massa Dawkins violated them without their say. We couldn't say no to a white man who wanted us for their pleasure. We were like human chattel; Massa would mate us with other slaves just like they did their stock.

Massa's affections towards his slave gals wasn't discussed. It was a crime for a slave to tell who was the father of a Colored woman's child. On the other hand, the rape of an enslaved woman by a white plantation owner or one of his friends was not considered a crime (Finkelman, 1997). The practice of the plantation owner fathering children with enslaved women was well known. They did it to increase the number of laborers on the plantation, but they also did it for pleasure. You tell me which is worse.

In December 1662, Virginia's colonial government enacted one of the first slave codes contradicting established common law. In the Act, it was determined that children born of an Englishman (white man) and a negro woman would follow the condition of the child's mother (Finkelman, 1997).

Slavery and Early Evangelism

I 'member when Ole Bessy would tell stories about Africans who came to the plantation. They would speak words none of them understood. They prayed to their own gods and would do

The Water Spirit
Mami Wata - Mother Water
(Courtesy National Museum of
African Art)

dances and sing songs in their own language. They never wanted to stay put and was always looking to run but didn't know where they were goin'. I recollect when they was dancing and singing and shouting, "Mami Wata! Mami Wata!" (Drewal, 2008). We would watch as they looked crazy to us. I remember wanting to learn what they were talking about. James—who had been on the plantation as long as Bessy—said he knew some of their words. His mama taught him words when he Africans who came to the plantation when she was captured. James say Mami Wata was a water spirit, like mother water. When the Africans would attend a baptism, they would start screaming, "Mami Wata! Mami Wata!"

I would sit as the local preacher would tell us that the African's words were voodoo and not the will of God, but we liked the way the Africans would sing, shout, and dance. There was always a leader that would sign some words, and then the others would repeat it, *lining a hymn* (Spencer, 1992). There was a rhythm to the song and a flow to the words. We did not know what they were saying, but it was easy to learn because of the way everything rolled. We started taking what the Africans did and doing it at our Sunday services and in the field when we worked. We were able to make the hard days in the field go a little faster while telling our own stories and dancing in a circle as we clapped and shuffled our feet. We would find whatever we could to fashion a drum or tambourine or use a washboard, and, if we were lucky, a fiddle. Others would use ring shouts as a form of hidden communication between the conductors (leaders) and those escaping bondage (the passengers) traveling along the Underground Railroad (Jacobs & Jones, 2019). We were forbidden to learn to read or write, and much of our communication came in the form of songs.

Class and Color
Within American Slavery

Plantation life unintentionally created a social order among the Coloreds on the plantation. Those who worked in the Big House and the mulattos were at the top of the system, with the drivers and artisans in the middle and the field workers and the darker-skinned Coloreds at the bottom of the social order (Hall, 2012). The social class system created for the Africans in America during enslavement persisted well after the abolishment of slavery (Bonilla-Silva, 2004). What became known as the "Blue Vein Society" emerged in northern states where Coloreds with higher percentages of Caucasian in them began to separate themselves from the larger Colored society. Many in this "society" looked more white than Black (Russell, Wilson, & Hall, 1993).

The real or perceived separation bread distrust between the groups even though Coloreds were viewed as less than human in general and three-fifths of a person at best (Jensen, 2014).

After a period in the field, I joined the others in the Big House and was no longer subjected to the grind of fieldwork. While both were enslaved, field workers often felt that the house workers were not to be trusted as they held valued positions and were more loyal to Massa than other Coloreds.

I remember new Africans didn't show up on the plantation no more (Eltis, 2007). Overseer Meeks began matching enslaved women and men, telling them they were to mate and make chillun even if they were promised to another. It was rumored that to encourage childbearing, some owners promised enslaved women their freedom after they had produced fifteen chillun (Smithers, 2012). I remember Colored women as young as thirteen would be expected to have chillun to increase the number of workers for their massas. By the age of twenty, many of the women on the plantation had five or more chillun. The enslaved would father some of the babies, while others would be fathered by their massas or one of the overseers. It was hard for us women because even if we jumped the broom and was married to the man we loved, we could still be forced to have relations with another slave man, the overseer, or anyone else Massa said. There were times when Massa or overseers like Meeks would determine which two people to breed, believing their offspring would be of the best stock (Smithers, 2012).

Voices In Our Blood

One night, Coffey took me to a stateroom in the Big House, apart from the house slaves. Some of the Colored maids took me to the bath to wash. Then Massa Dawkins came in. Massa made several overtures toward me, all of which I rejected. He wanted me to submit of my own free will. So, he made the offer more appealing, promising to make me a washwoman so I would never work in the field again. Once, he got so impatient that he threatened to sell me off as a field hand to the worst plantation he could find (Smithers, 2012). I once again rejected his sexual advances but without success. He took me as a housekeeper and mistress, ultimately giving birth to my first child, Randle (1825), who was fathered by Bill Dawkins. Most of the other women had several chillun by the time my baby was born. Over the years, I had five more chillun with Massa: Nancie (1833), Ned (1834), Sallie (1835), Betsy (1852), and Hannah (1859).

The census records for Coloreds during slavery and the reconstruction era were maintained with less vigor than those of whites (Evans, 1962). In the family's oral

Arthur Vaughn

history, the years of Betsy and Hannah's birth have been in question. If accurate, Katy would have been in her 50s and Bill in his 60s at the time of their deliveries.

My boy Randle looked like his pappy. People who did not know he was my baby thought of him as white. It was common knowledge who Randle's pappy was, but it wasn't openly discussed. Massa was known to father a mess of chillun with enslaved women. It was believed Miss Milley bore ten chillun and Rosetta eight chillun from ole Bill Dawkins. Of the twenty-four chillun between the three of us, we were not sure how many of our chillun were fathered by Massa and how many may have been fathered by a man who was courting us on the plantation. To save face in the community, Massa would tell his brothers he did not want anything to do with jezebel-colored women. Bill's suggestion that the women who bore his children were somehow promiscuous brought pain and embarrassment to us. The truth was, I bedded Bill and no other man.

Sex was not taken lightly by the enslaved community, and having children outside of marriage was considered an act against the community. Slave culture included its own sexual standards driven by African tradition and influenced by Christianity. Still, slave women that gave birth outside of wedlock were not treated with the same disdain as white women who did the same (Gaspar & Hine, 1996).

I 'member Bill telling his brothers' wives that we were having relations with everyone who would have us—that he could never keep track of who we were bedding and who fathered all of our chillun. This was not true. Massa never wanted the outside to know he was the one having his way with us and that our babies were his. The white community would have considered Bill's act a profound sin against the church and God. Bill's reputation in the community would have been forever tarnished, and his influence would have been diminished (Schwartz, 2009).

Massa's use of the enslaved for sexual pleasure was ignored and not spoken of, and open affection was unacceptable. Negro children were not treated as heirs but rather like any other piglet on the plantation. I would overhear other white men saying that Dawkins treated his coloreds too good. "They gonna start taking liberties and acting up if he's not careful," they would say. While Bill's actions were concerning, the community dared not openly voice their contempt because they relied on Bill Dawkins' wealth and political power. There were times when I would see two beautiful children playing together—one white and the other Colored, both sisters. We saw white daughters marry men knowing they had fathered children with enslaved women (Schwartz, 2009).

Though Bill had chillun with many of his housekeepers, Rosetta and Milley's children were treated with additional favoritism. Their mothers had always been house servants, and Milley was the head of the house, directing all the washerwomen, wet nurses, cooks, and butlers. When Massa Dawkins hosted other white families at his plantation, it was clear who was running things, as everyone at the event saw Massa Dawkins defer to Milley as if she was the woman of the house. Milley essentially ran the day-to-day of their massa's home and directed the work of other enslaved workers in the same manner the white overseer and a negro driver would in the field. Massa Dawkins' kin did not like how the enslaved at Bill's plantation moved freely and spoke more openly in the presence of white people. Southern tradition during this period was built on custom. The enslaved were considered inferior and were never allowed to interact with their masters the way Bill allowed some of his enslaved to do.

The Slave Master's Colored Son

Since my boy Randle was also Massa Dawkins' son, he had privileges that other slave chillun weren't provided. As a periodic house servant and part-time artisan, Randle was treated more like a pet. He was well-dressed and of decent manners. Being born and bred in the Dawkins family, along with the constant association with his massa and his massa's family, led to such an implied attachment ensuring good treatment. I watched my son Randle make a way for himself. I 'members when he was a little boy running round the Big House and away from the overseer's whip. Randle was always at his pappy's side.

As he grew, he was taught how to shoe horses and worked in the mill and ironworks, which kept him out of the fields. Massa Dawkins saw to it that Randle learned to read and write (Monaghan,1998). The other Coloreds on the plantation knew the enslaved weren't supposed to do these things. I feared for my child every day. Massa Dawkins would tell Randle:

"Boy, I am teaching you things a Colored should not know. No one is to know you can read or write. If another white man learns you can do these things, they may kill you on sight. I want you to use what I am showing you to teach the other Colored the words of the Good Book. Ephesians 6:5-12, Slaves, obey your earthly masters with respect and fear, and with sincerity of heart, just as you would obey Christ" (Barker, Strauss, Brown, Blomberg & Williams, 2020). Boy, it is your job to help Mr. Meeks and Coffey to keep the other Coloreds in line."

I 'member Massa telling Randle that he was to help teach the Good Word on Sundays and let Meeks know who the troublemakers were. Folks that did not obey the rules or started problems were sold off to other plantations.

I remember seeing new Coloreds coming to the plantation straight from Africa, but Randle never seen the pain Africans on American shores experienced. Randle perceived the conditions of slavery through the eyes of his privilege and book learning. My baby understood that he owed his place in life to Massa. He watched people who looked like him suffer from the lash at the hand of the overseer Meeks and driver Coffey at times, but all he knew was black folk born here. I watched as my baby grew angrier every day and more distant from Massa. He would spend more time around the fields and watched what others were subjected to and the living conditions of the so-called Colored in America.

Massa took Randle and other favored Coloreds with him to pick up supplies for the plantation and to slave auctions like he once took Coffey. I didn't understand, but I watched as Randle began to see that the enslaved could be more than their current condition. I believe the book learning that Bill gave to Randle and his traveling from place to place with Massa changed my boy. Randle said he saw free Coloreds and understood conversations and writings that no one else on the plantation understood. He heard how white men feared the increase in runaway slaves and how some whites wanted to put an end to slavery. He would talk with me about these things. I knew nothing, but slavery and his talk scared me.

"Randle, Massa Dawkins is good to us, boy. Don't be sharing these fool notions of running with your brothers and sisters. You need to just get running out of your mind. Dem slave patrols be killing Coloreds who dare attempt escape (Reichel, 1988). When white folks think you is uppity or a troublemaker, they be whipping them thoughts out ya, or worse, they be selling ya black butt off. I 'members seeing Coloreds being sold along with horses and cattle on Massa's plantation."

I would tell him stories I dun heard of how white men whipped the skin and even killed enslaved folks for trying to escape. White men be watchin' for anyone who had the notion to try to escape. I could tell that no matter what I said, Randle continued to dream of running to freedom. I would say, "Randle, I watched them burn Henry during the middle of a party and made us other slaves watch just cause a white woman say he looked at

Courtesy A.D. Vaughn Collection

her wrong" (Paton, 2001). He would tell tales of Black Moses and how she was taking folks away from they massas and getting them up north where they be free.

Black Moses was the name given to Harriet Tubman by abolitionist William Lloyd Garrison because of her work in leading the enslaved to freedom through the Underground Railroad (Singer, A., 2012).

I was so happy my boy never took off, but Coffey caught wind of what he was sayin' and told Meeks about what he dun said. For the first time, I had to watch my boy get punished. My boy got the lash from Mr. Meeks' whip, and Massa Dawkins never said a word. Massa had promised me that my chillun would never get whooped. Massa lied!

Massa was trying to get thoughts of escaping out of Randle's head. He thought if Randle knew the pain of the whip or if he had a woman, he would stop talking 'bout escaping. There was a slave gal Massa had his eye on that he had purchased from old man Pierson. Old man Pierson owned a smaller plantation nearby but needed more bucks to work the fields. Them enslaved gals just didn't get as much work done. Massa figured Pierson's gal, Phoebe, was right for breeding and might settle Randle down. So, we went down to Pierson's place and bought her. I 'member seeing this gal in Massa Pierson's fields when I was rented out to their plantation in the winter, but I didn't know much about her.

Women Named Phoebe

Around the age of twenty-six, Bill Dawkins matched Randle with a negro woman from the Pierson plantation in hopes of getting his illegitimate son to end his notions of running. Massa had say over who his slaves was matched with. So, the next Sunday, Randle and Phoebe Pierson jumped the broom down by the river and were married.

While we were happy for them, we knew the white folks had say over us (West, 2004). If Randle caused trouble, Mr. Meeks or Massa might punish him and make his wife bed some other man. Or if a white man fancied Phoebe, he might ask Massa to have his way with her. We was Massa's to do what he pleased, and we never forgot it.

Their marriage suggested that Randle was now tied to the plantation and the way of life that came with it. However, 'cause of Randle's ways, he would increasingly be subject to abuse at the hands of Meeks. He no longer lived in the Big House, and his quarters was searched for guns, swords, and other weapons that could be used for escape or an armed rebellion. Massa could no longer trust Randle as he did before, so he sent his boy to the field. The law said we could strike a white man to defend the Massa's life but was forbidden from doing so to protect our own life. Any white man could punish, arrest, or kill us if we didn't obey them. We had seen that for ourselves. My boy never stopped dreaming of freedom, but with his new wife, Phoebe Pierson, his energy turned from his own independence to how he could help others to freedom as a conductor on the Underground Railroad.

Moses Dawkins
(Courtesy A.D. Vaughn Collection)

Not long after they was married, Phoebe Pierson welcomed their first child, Moses, into the world, in 1853. We can only wonder if they chose the name Moses because of Randle's admiration for Harriett "Black Moses" Tubman and his desire to lead other Coloreds to freedom. Moses had three sons and two daughters. Moses Dawkins died at the age of 120 on March 15, 1973. During the marriage, Randle and Phoebe Pierson had ten children––four sons and six daughters. They named their fifth child after her mother. Phoebe Dawkins was born in 1860, a year before the War for Southern Independence began (Stromberg, 1979).

Phoebe Dawkins lived on the Dawkins plantation. She knew her grandfather had been Massa Dawkins. Much of her life was

Phoebe (Dawkins) Hill was the daughter of Randle Dawkins and Phoebe Pierson. (A.D. Vaughn Collection)

50

spent toiling in the fields and experiencing the lash of the whip. She never knew what it was like to be an artisan like her father or live in the Big House like her grandmother, Katy.

Arthur Vaughn

The Storm Before the Storm

Over the years, overseer Meeks became increasingly harsh as slave numbers grew on the plantation. I believe he was scared 'cause there were so many more of us Coloreds than white folks, and we began hearing tales of slaves killing white folks. Massa Dawkins' slaves began running, and Massa blamed Meeks for not keeping control over us. We could see that Coffey was getting old. He feared a lot of the young folk and was more treacherous than ever. The threats of escape increased, as did the worries about rebellion, calling for increased fear and violence by overseers.

Folks like Meeks were proud of their work, and any comforts we enjoyed were at his whim. It wasn't uncommon for an overseer, drivers, and even the enslaver himself to punish the free Colored or the enslaved for perceived wrongdoing with ten or more lashes with a raw-hide whip (Franklin & Schweninger, 2000). Those handing out punishment might laugh or smile at the Colored. The free or enslaved could often be heard crying out, "Oh, Massa, please stop! Please stop, sur! Oh, Lawd, save me!"

One hot June evening, Bill had all of us get the plantation ready for this grand affair he was planning. There were plantation owners from Rock Hill to the Santee and Aiken to Charleston, all coming to talk about something the Yankees were trying to make them do. We could tell it was serious business by the way Massa, Mr. Meeks, and the other white men were carrying on. They was talking about something called an abolitionist. They spoke of people who did not want slavery in places I had never heard about.

There was a lot of yelling, and I heard words I didn't understand. Bill Dawkins and his friends met to determine what to do about these folk who were fighting the spread of slavery to the western territories. Southerners feared if these abolitionists took over, the only way of life they had ever known would be crushed. The actions of the new-formed Liberty Party were not to go unchallenged (Bretz, 1929).

Massa Dawkins and other slave owners were what was called a Democrat. They didn't want to be told what to do in how they ran their plantations or what was done in their states. They did not want the President and his friends to decide if there could be slavery in any state. As a southern Democrat or Dixiecrat, as they were known, their family was tied to racial segregation and forced servitude (Wagner & Fish, 2007). Southern enslavers increasingly expressed fears about uprisings like the insurrection in the French colony of St. Domingue, which resulted in the bloody process and the founding of the nation now known as Haiti (Geggus, 2012).

Over the years, Bill's holdings in enslaved Africans and crops grew while his brothers showed not to have the same head for business or simply squandered their wealth. Bill Dawkins' brothers understood that they needed slaves to run their farms.

They did not want free Coloreds; they did not want race mixing; they did not want anyone telling them how to live. They believed the Dawkins family could expand its wealth and political influence through marriage. They wanted Bill to marry the daughter of another wealthy family. Bill's kin understood that his marrying could strengthen their extended family's position in South Carolina and the region (Reed, 1988).

Things were different on the plantation these days. People were more afraid and nervous. I ain't never seen white men acting so troubled. I remember hearing more stories about runaways than ever before. Meeks had Coffey rounding up tools, spikes, and pitchforks at the end of each day. They would search the quarters down in the slave area to make sure no one had things that could be used as weapons. I remember tales about them offering extra food to those who told on folks planning to escape and whipping them if they didn't tell. I became more and more worried about Randle because I knew freedom was burning in him.

As the calendar turned to 1860, there were 4 million enslaved Africans in the United States, and 400,000 of them—10 percent— lived in South Carolina. Coloreds, enslaved and free, made up 57 percent of the state's population (Forret, 2016).

Rebellions by white abolitionists increasingly included free and previously enslaved Coloreds. Runaway attempts were increasing, and protests against slavery by groups, including the Quakers and Mennonites, were becoming more common. The atmosphere around the nation was anxious. At the turn of the decade, the states whose economic engine was built on the backs of slaves felt a revolutionary political power shift that favored ending slavery (Snodgrass, 2015).

"Am I Not a Man and a Brother?" became an international symbol of the abolitionist movement. (Courtesy Library of Congress)

Arthur Vaughn

The Cross of Redemption

Unknown to Massa Dawkins, dissension was increasing on his plantation, led by Randle. Massa thought teaching my boy to read would be a good thing. He never expected book learning would lead to Randle helping folk run away. I would watch my boy sit in the field, looking up to the sky and watching the eagles fly. I often wondered if Randle wished he had wings so he could take off and soar. Every day I was happy my boy didn't attempt to escape his lot in life.

As a child, Randle would travel around the South with Massa, Meeks, or Coffey to purchase goods and, at times, buy new slaves to work at the plantation. Randle saw one way to be free was to take advantage of the ins and outs of the Dawkins plantation to help runaways make it north to freedom. Because of his unrecognized but understood position as the son of Bill Dawkins, he was permitted movement around the grounds with fewer restrictions than the other Coloreds. He used this "freedom" to identify hiding places and paths for those seeking to escape bondage through self-emancipation.

Black Moses sent word through song and tale that slaves seeking freedom should run from their massas to the north. The Underground Railroad was a network of safe houses and transportation provided by abolitionists for the enslaved who sought freedom (Foner, 2015). I remember the day Randle told us that he heard white men talking about something called the Fugitive Slave Act (Basinger, 2003 & Lennon, 2016). He say they had people who would go to the north and bring black folks who ran away back to they massas. He say runaways had to go to some place called Canada if they wanted to be free. He heard slaves was running away to

Fugitive Slave Act Poster
(Courtesy National Archives)

somewhere called Missouri on their way north, but he did not know where that was. He say if runaways traveled along the Mississippi River bank, they could cross a river in Missouri to gain freedom in Illinois (Nolen, 2003).

The Meachum's home on Fourth Street in St. Louis was a safe house on the Underground Railroad. From there, they helped enslaved people escape to Illinois—a Free State where slavery was outlawed. On the night of May 21, 1855, in the area that is now part of the Mississippi Greenway: Riverfront Trail north of the Merchant's Bridge, Mary Meachum attempted to help a small group of enslaved people cross the Mississippi River to Illinois, where slavery was outlawed. However, enslavers and law enforcement officials caught at least five of the enslaved people and arrested Mary for her participation in the plot. She was charged in criminal court for helping the "fugitives" escape (Great Rivers Greenway, 2023).

Mary Meachum Mural at St. Louis Great Rivers Greenway
(A.D. Vaughn Collection)

The Price of the Ticket

One thing Bill Dawkins enjoyed more than money was the power and influence over state matters that their position provided him. The actions throughout the states were being felt on the Dawkins plantation. The community looked for Bill Dawkins, one of its largest holders of land and human property, to lead the charge for the protection of its way of life. Bill would not let his friends down.

"Randle, get the buggy ready. We are going on a trip," I heard Massa Dawkins call out.

This morning was particularly frightening. The clouds were a mixture of an ominous gray and black. Off in the distance, it looked as if the clouds and the ground met with no sky between them. The plantation was silent, and the wind stood still.

"Put ya Sunday meeting clothes on, Randle. I have a meeting with Vice President Breckinridge."

I was afraid for my boy. While Massa expected him to keep the other enslaved folk in line, Randle was preaching freedom and encouraging folks to run. I was fearful one of the treacherous Coloreds was gonna tell Meeks or Coffey, and my boy would be met with the lash again or, even worse, hung. Massa was blind to Randle's ways and still held him close, even though Randle was spying on him from right by his side. From his pappy, he learned the ways white folk tried to capture runaways and the traps used on the plantation to find out who was planning against Dawkins.

The trip to see Vice President Breckinridge was abnormally quiet without Randle's singing and typical jovial quips. Everyone knew the mood on the Dawkins plantation was changing. Breckinridge was a southern democrat who firmly believed the federal government should not intervene in maintaining the practice of slavery (Brown, Tager, Handlin, & O'Connor, 2015; Heck, 1955).

After arriving at the Breckinridge plantation, there were two separate and distinct conversations. Bill was pledging his and other South Carolinian voters' support to Breckinridge, while Randle met with the enslaved who yearned to be free and were planning escape routes north to Canada. Randle had shared his plans with me before he and Massa left. I always fretted that my boy was going to be found out. I knew what happened to slaves who ran. I 'members seeing folks hobbled where they could no longer walk right. We seen folks branded with R's on their face and others who would have half a foot chopped off (Keefer, 2019). I could not imagine what Massa would do to Randle if he was found out.

When my baby come home to me, I cried and cried my eyes out.

He said, "There, there, Mama. You ain't gotta worry about me."

My boy had grown up. He told me stories about things they saw and stories he heard from the other plantations they visited along the way. He told me that Bill seemed different, even a little scared about what was to come, but then calmed after meeting with the vice president. I did not know what any of that meant. I was just happy my boy was home.

Soon, Randle and Bill were off again—this time to Charleston, but this was different. Dawkins' nephews and Coffey went with them. Over the years, the younger Dawkins brothers were in varying states of poor health. While Bill had not married and had no legitimate heirs, his brothers married and had their own sons. I feared they were on to Randle's dealings and took Coffey to keep watch.

Randle kept to himself, listened to what folks were saying, and watched what was happening. Coffey was always watching and didn't let him out of his sight. Coffey had grown old, and Randle wasn't afraid of him anymore. However, he knew Bill's kinfolk did not like the comforts he was afforded and would take any opportunity to punish Randle. The brothers knew Randle was Bill's child, and every time they saw my boy, they were infuriated. They believed he and Bill's other bastards should have been sold off long ago.

This trip wasn't to get more slaves but some big meeting to pick the president. Randle told me there was much arguing about things he didn't understand. The Dixiecrats understood that if Republican Abraham Lincoln was elected president, the states' autonomy would be challenged.

The Dixiecrats, as they were called, were Southern Democrats who strongly believed in states' rights and Southern cultural preservation, which included support for racial segregation (Barnard, 1984; Newman, 2002).

Arthur Vaughn

Blues for Mister Charlie

In 1860, the same year Randle Dawkins and Phoebe Pierson's daughter, Phoebe, was born, Abraham Lincoln was elected the 16th President of the United States. With the election of Lincoln, many Southerners saw a real and present threat to the survival of slavery, the foundation of the Southern way of life. Some wealthy slave owners supported secession from the Union, viewing Lincoln's elections as a threat to their prosperous way of life. With Randle in tow again, Bill Dawkins attended the South Carolina secession convention at South Carolina Institute Hall in Charleston.

> *"The issue before the country is the extinction of slavery. The Southern states are now in the crisis of their fate, and if we read aright the signs of the times, nothing is needed for our deliverance but that the ball of revolution be set in motion."*
> *— Charleston Mercury on November 3, 1860*

Charles Pinckney, who served in the House of Representatives from 1819-1821, previously warned those who would listen that economic interests of the North and South were at odds. He further believed slavery was the only question that could separate the Union. He stated that a consequence of the Missouri Compromise "may be the division of this union and a civil war." (Gary, 2004).

On December 20, 1860, South Carolina became the first state to secede from the Union. The counter-revolutionary act by South Carolina gained support, and two months later, they were joined by Georgia, Alabama, Mississippi, Florida, Louisiana, and Texas to form the Confederate States of America. The United States of America was no more. The effect of the acts of political aggression by the former Dixiecrats reverberated through the former colonies. Southern militia began attacks on federal forts, including Fort Sumter in Charleston, marking the beginning of the War for Southern Independence (Cauthen, 2005).

Life on the plantation changed after the war started. We saw young and old white men from around here join the Confederate cause, including Dawkins' nephews. During the war, the Dawkins' plantation served as one site for prisoner camps. The plantation also provided textiles, food, and uniforms to the war effort. Us women made uniforms and blankets for the soldiers while the men in the mills were making weapons. Old men like Meeks would watch over the making of knives and such to make sure none went missing. I was more afraid for Randle and my other chillun than ever before. We hear tell of Union troops coming, but we never saw one Yankee soldier until after the war.

During this period, Randle led many escape attempts at the Dawkins plantation. Word got to Meeks that a group of Coloreds planned to escape one night. When our long-time overseer and some slave patrols tried to stop 'em, Meeks found himself on the wrong side of a blade. The death of overseer Meeks brought further instability to the Dawkins plantation. Massa Dawkins lacked direct experience managing field hands, and the lack of qualified replacements for Meeks led to decreases in harvesting crops across the plantation.

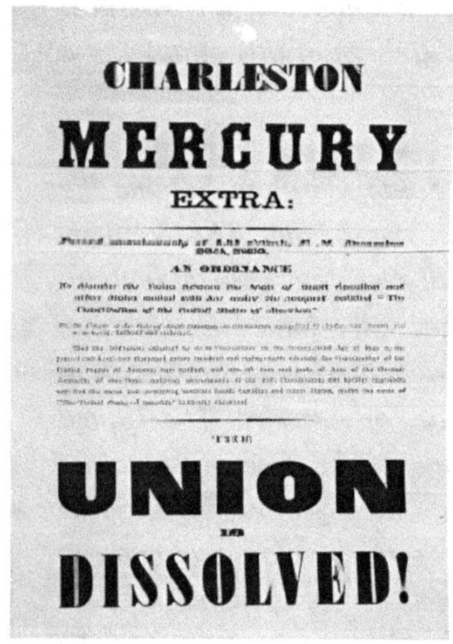

Courtesy South Carolina Historical Society

My boy Randle was more headstrong than ever. With all this confusion, Randle would help guide runaways to marshy areas along the Combahee River, stretching from the Yemassee area through Beaufort, where free Colored communities were established. This period also saw an increasing number of escaped Coloreds joining the federal troops in their fight to liberate others. At the height of the war, an estimated 180,000 Colored men served in the Union Army fighting against the Confederacy (Blassingame, 1965).

President Abraham Lincoln issued the Emancipation Proclamation on January 1, 1863, as the nation approached its third year of bloody civil war. The proclamation declared that "all persons held as slaves within the rebellious states are and henceforward shall be free." (Lincoln, 2015).

After deliverance in 1863, southern Coloreds were disenfranchised, exploited by former slave owners and subjected to harsh forms of violence (Adamson, 1983). In a daily struggle for survival, the Colored woman found no time for pedestals or social chatter. The struggle to survive shaped the Colored woman's existence while the white woman was imprisoned by the sexist notion of what a woman's place was at the time. The Colored woman was subject to rape at the hands of Colored and white men and had to use talents and skills at all levels. The treatment of Colored women was born out of slave labor practices and eroded womanhood for this population of human beings. The Colored woman found themselves victims of hypocrisy. They were not protected by custom or law, but if they defied the law by lashing out at their attacker, they could be fatally condemned by being shot or hung (McKittrick, 2006). Just as during enslavement, aggressors would argue that the action was consensual or resulted from the negro woman's lustful nature. During this period, women—both Colored and white—relied heavily on men to provide for them and their children. So, they were limited to work as the domestics or performing agricultural work (Gaspar & Hine, 1996).

With the loss of so many South Carolinians during the war and the freeing of the formerly enslaved, Dawkins was surprisingly able to maintain land the family previously held.

Even Bill's financial support for the war and his help rebuilding the region prevented the growing contempt his nephews had for him. Massa Dawkins was an enslaver but perceived to be less entrenched in the culture of slavery than others. Dawkins viewing his offspring as free Blacks living in South Carolina inflamed others who wished to maintain pre-war culture and practices. During this time, Coloreds were commonly referred to by the whites in their community as *Bill Dawkins' Free Niggers*.

With the assassination of President Lincoln less than a week after the end of the Civil War, Lincoln's successor, Andrew Jackson, pardoned Bill Dawkins and other Confederate sympathizers for their actions in support of the war. Newly installed President Jackson then quickly moved to restore power in the south to Confederate loyalists. South Carolina and other southern states quickly moved to create

William Dawkins Civil War Presidential Pardon (A.D. Vaughn Collection)

what became known as Black Codes, designed to control the formerly enslaved and to ensure they worked for the benefit of white land and business owners (Mungo, 2009).

Sonny's Blues

Randle moved his family off their plantation, where he attempted to use his expertise doing mill and iron work to avoid the harsh plantation life he witnessed during legalized slavery. However, the newly enacted Black Codes made Randle's endeavors illegal. South Carolina and most southern states passed laws intended to control the movement and actions of Coloreds (Mungo, 2009). The law in South Carolina went as far as to state that "No person of color shall pursue or practice the art, trade, or business of an artisan, mechanic or shop-keeper, or any other trade, employment, or business (besides that of husbandry or that of a servant under a contract for service or labor) on his own account and for his own benefit, or in partnership with a white person, or as agent or servant of any persons until he shall have obtained a license therefore from the Judge of the District Court, which license shall be good for one year only." (Mungo, 2009).

The new laws prevented Randle from independently performing his trade, and he found himself back on the Dawkins plantation working for Massa Dawkins' nephew, Spencer, who assumed control of the plantation after the end of the Civil War. Randle's work helping Coloreds escape to freedom may have been over, but his work to ensure his fellow Coloreds were afforded the rights guaranteed by the Emancipation Proclamation and the 14th Amendment to the United States Constitution continued. This was dangerous work as the rise of white supremacists and other homegrown terror groups like the Ku Klux Klan (The Klan) were on the rise.

The Klan grew as part of a counter-revolutionary movement designed to combat the Republican Party's Reconstruction-era policies aimed at establishing political and economic equality for the Colored (Bullard, 1998). Ku Klux Klan members included farmers, laborers, lawyers, merchants, physicians, and ministers.

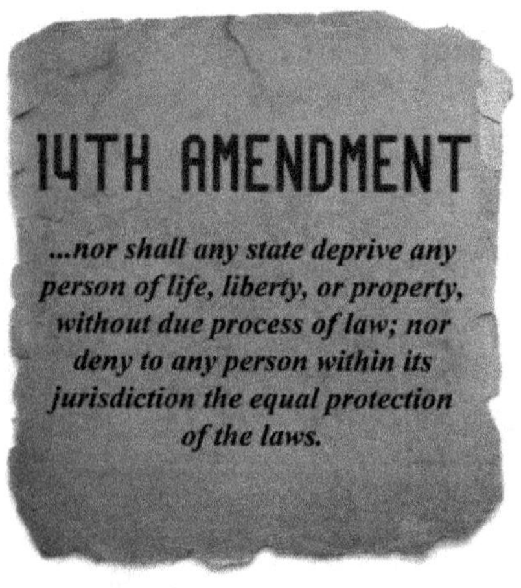

A.D. Vaughn Collection

One fall evening, Randle called out to his wife, Phoebe, telling her to hide under the bed in the backroom. Members of the Klan, draped in white sheets, circled the shotty wood cabin they lived in on the Dawkins plantation. It was hard not to suspect Spencer Dawkins of condoning and even encouraging these actions. Spencer had played with Randle as a child and knew they were kin but refused to acknowledge his blood relationship to his Colored cousin.

The Klan members screamed to Randle, "Nigra, y'all gonna stop causing trouble and riling up our Colored folks!"

Gunshots rang out, startling the other Coloreds. Phoebe screamed in fear for her and her husband's life. The Klan not only wanted to scare Randle but also stamp out the fight in any of Randle's followers in their fight for equal rights.

But Randle wouldn't stop. He kept speaking to anyone who would listen and was not shy about letting folks know he was the one helping the formerly enslaved escape to freedom. His relentlessness further enraged the white community, and he feared his death by hanging or gun violence was imminent. Still, he continued to speak to parishioners at Methodist churches and talked with those who worshiped on the Dawkins plantation. Some of the flock would later be given permission to start their own church, which became Paradise AME Church and sat on the same land where Katy, Randle, and Phoebe Dawkins were once enslaved.

Slavery at the hands of individuals had been abolished through legislative action and war, but debt slavery or debt servitude persisted (Daniel, 1972). Many plantation owners could not manage their land or bring in crops without workers they previously held in bondage. These plantation owners created a system of tenant farming and sharecropping where the formerly enslaved could work the land of the plantation owner for a fee, and they were to share in the profits.

Paradise African Methodist Episcopal Church was founded after the Civil War by those formerly enslaved on the Dawkins Planation. The rebuilt structure is located at 115 Paradise Church Rd, Union, SC 29379. (A.D. Vaughn Collection)

Arthur Vaughn

Most Coloreds did not understand the agreements they were entering into and, at the end of a harvest, were told they had not met the terms of the agreement and thus still owed a debt to the landowner. These debt contracts were enforced, prohibiting the Coloreds from leaving and creating a new form of involuntary service called peonage (Shlomowitz, 1979). Black Codes allowed the landowners to be referred to as masters and those entering into the contracts to be referred to as servants. These codes returned many of the thousands of Colored people who remained in the South into an environment that resembled enslavement (Mungo, 2009). Limiting the movement, actions, and behaviors of the previously enslaved was paramount to preserving the economic wealth and social order in the South. During this period, the laborers would not show up on any ledger indicating they were property but were, in many ways, subjected to the same inhumane practices that occurred during the antebellum period (Adamson, 1983).

Seven years after the end of the war, William Dawkins died on August 7, 1872. After the death of William, his last will and testament was read. In his will, he referred to the offspring that he treated as enslaved as his children. His will listed two of his enslaved wives, Milley and Rosetta, and their daughters as the recipients of the balance of his approximately 1,300 acres of land, crops, livestock, farming tools, wagons, and one-third of the cotton crop, subtracting 700

William Dawkins was buried at Salem Presbyterian Church Cemetery in Fairfield County, South Carolina (A.D. Vaughn Collection)

acres to be given to his nephew, Spencer Dawkins. Katy was notably left out of Bill Dawkins' last will and testament. There is no record of why Massa Dawkins left Katy out of the will, but it is assumed he found out about Randle's betrayal and wasn't going to reward his treachery.

Nothing Personal

Spencer, Bill's nephew, was named the executor of the will. Because of the Black Codes enacted across the South and the sense that Coloreds remained inferior to whites, Spencer chose not to abide by all the terms of the will. Spencer was raised to believe enslavement was a system of labor, wealth, power, and politics. While freedom may have been the law, changing the behavior of the enslavers and the enslaved was difficult.

Like many formerly enslaved, Miley and Rosetta were unaware of their rights, and the Black Codes system made it difficult for Coloreds to prevail in court. The beneficiaries of the Dawkins estate remained in servitude at the plantation until 1879 when, with the assistance of a sympathetic attorney, a petition was filed in Probate Court in Union County. To this point, Coloreds had not found an ally in southern courts. This was even more challenging as this case was brought by two formerly enslaved women against a white man, Spencer Dawkins. Citing the 14th Amendment of the United States Constitution, enacted in 1868, the judge ruled in favor of the formerly enslaved women. The particular section of the

Amendment used by the Dawkins' women's attorney spoke to the due process clause:

"All persons born or naturalized in the United States, and subject to the jurisdiction thereof, are citizens of the United States and the state wherein they reside. No state shall make or enforce any law which shall abridge the privileges or immunities of citizens of the United States; nor shall any state deprive any person of life, liberty, or property without due process of law, nor deny to any person within its jurisdiction the equal protection of the laws" **(Pusey, 2016).**

This legal victory was a major accomplishment then, and the formerly enslaved throughout the South rejoiced when learning of it. It was believed that on this day, the Confederate roses that adorned the fountain in front of the Dawkins plantation bloomed, the sky was clear, and the sun shined bright (Blythe, 2012). Katy Dawkins worked in the fields alongside other formerly enslaved Coloreds and poor whites as a tenant farmer until her death in 1881. Unfortunately, Milley also died in 1881, followed by Rosetta in 1885. Both women took to their graves the knowledge that their families would be free and that they had won their battle to have

Colored descendants of William Dawkins served as members of the Steward and Trustee Boards when Paradise AME Church was rebuilt (A.D. Vaughn Collection)

the same rights as their former enslavers. Their heirs retained control of the land and all rents and profits made from the land as indicated in William Dawkins' original will. In 1966, a rebuilt Paradise AME church was erected on the land next to the gravesites of various Colored descendants of the Dawkins family.

The Long Reconstruction:
The Post Civil War South

Radical Reconstruction

Rosa Mae Hill, circa 1990.
Granddaughter of Pompey Hill
and Phoebe Dawkins
(A.D. Vaughn Collection)

B orn on March 13, 1911, I am the great-granddaughter of Randle Dawkins, Rosa Mae Hill. I suffered through the Jim Crow South and the segregated North and have lived through two World Wars, the Korean War, and the Vietnam War. I was a young adult during the depression years. I participated in the Women's Liberation Movement, and during the 50s, 60s, and 70s, I participated in the Civil Rights Movement. I witnessed women and Blacks become full citizens when we were awarded the right to vote. I've been Colored, Negro, Black, and African American (Martin, 1991; Smith, 1992) and blessed to see the turn of a new century.

My grandfather, Pompey Hill, was born into slavery in South Carolina on August 4, 1857. Pompey was born along the river where Chester and Union counties meet, in Fishdam Ford. Countless narratives about Pompey suggested that he was known as a traveling man and made his way toward Bill Dawkins' plantation after emancipation. Pompey found himself working odd jobs and helping on various plantations to make a way for himself.

After the Civil War, things were difficult for everyone. Southern whites' attitudes towards the recently freed Colored didn't change just because the Confederacy was defeated. No one truly knew what this meant for the slave owner or the former enslaved. Centuries of social norms would not instantly evaporate because Old Abe said so (Williams, 1946). Losses from the war once focused on the Federal Union Army turned toward the newly freed Blacks. According to Pop, lynching became commonplace as a fear tactic and form of punishment. In the states that once succeeded from the Union, Jim Crow laws were passed to discriminate against the once enslaved, creating a "separate but equal" system of living (Mungo, 2009).

Fear of being jailed or killed kept many Colored people in line in the South. In southern states, incarcerated African American women performed backbreaking labor on chain gangs alongside Black men (Paton, 2001).

Like my paternal great-grandfather Randle, my grandfather Pompey risked his freedom and life for the freedom of the southern Colored. Randle Dawkins had been a conductor on the Underground Railroad and took in Pompey when he arrived at the Dawkins plantation. After a time, Randle promised Grandma Phoebe to Pompey, and they were married. The idea that a Colored man could promise his daughters to another without the woman's consent seemed to be a byproduct derived from the tradition of slave masters deciding who enslaved women would breed with (Smithers, 2012).

Grandma Phoebe and other Colored women in the South during their time did not enjoy the rights of freed Colored men and were not revered by the Colored man or others (Gaspar & Hine, 1996). Lessons from slavery were passed down after freedom. The Colored woman was taught her skin color was distasteful, and they were of limited intelligence but had tremendous strength and an insatiable sexual appetite (Gaspar & Hine, 1996). In contrast, white women were placed on pedestals, being largely confined to the home, the church, and polite society (Gaspar & Hine, 1996).

My aunt Mary was born in 1880, not long after Pompey and Phoebe Dawkins were married. The day she was born marks the day our first family member was born free in the United States. Benjamin Franklin Hill (Pop) was the second Dawkins baby to be born free three years later. Unfortunately, Pompey was viewed as a troublemaker by the white folks. The peckerwoods ran him out of his own home before he got the chance to see his firstborn son. Pompey was never heard from again. We like to believe they didn't kill him, too.

It was a dangerous time for Colored men after the Civil War. Our men were being legally killed at the hands of white men simply for being Black (Bullard, 1998). After Aunt Mary and Pop, Grandma Phoebe had two more children, William "Hence" Ruth (1886-1956) and John Sartor, Jr. (1892-1973). I never knew my grandmother's date of birth. In fact, Pop didn't know his exact birthday either. He figured he and his cousin, Madora Dawkins, were about the same age and that he was born around Thanksgiving time. He celebrated his birth on the 27th of November. From what he told me. I gather that his mother must have been relatively young when he was born.

Sadly, Grandma Phoebe did not live to see Pop become a man. He was around the age of fourteen when she passed away. After my grandmother's passing, Pop's sister, Mary Hill, took care of him as best she could. Pop's brothers, Hence and John, were taken in by their respective fathers after Grandma Phoebe's death. It is believed John's father was a wealthy white farmer and had a large family. Little was known about Hence's father other than his name was Henderson Ruth.

Papa Was a Rolling Stone

Even though Pop's sister, Mary, was taking care of him, he wandered from place to place doing as he pleased. He could not get along with his sister's husband, so he decided to hobo. Pop would tell us stories about how he was full of mischief as a boy. As teenagers, they had a knack for taking each other's girlfriends or would do something to let the other fellow know that such and such was their girlfriend.

Pop and Aunt Mary were talented at the mouth harp and impressed everyone at local dances. If something suspicious were going on at one of the dances, they would shoot out the lights and leave everyone in the dark. He said he got caught in the dark at one party and had no lantern to light the way. He could only guess where he was by the light in the distance. He was hurrying to get home, and with each step he took, he heard a *Zzz zzz* noise. He was so afraid that he walked faster, but the noise got faster, too. So, he started to run. Still, the noise continued. The faster he ran, the faster the noise became. *Zzz zzz zzz.* He finally realized it was his corduroy knickers. The knees would rub together as he walked. He was very much relieved.

Pop moved between Lexington, Union, and York counties in South Carolina by hitching on the backs of trains between the two stops. Eventually, he settled down in Rock Hill. Located in the north-central area of South Carolina, approximately twenty miles south of Charlotte, NC, Rock Hill was founded in 1852 when the railroad line was being constructed through the area. Irmo was a small farming community built around a water and refueling stop for trains traveling the Columbia, Newberry, and Laurens Railroad (Hollis, 1984). He was hoboing freight cars when he met a girl named Grace Nelson. Pop was supposed to be looking

Mary Hill married Henry Cook. They are pictured here. They had no children. Mary was the older sister of Benjamin Franklin Hill. Benjamin went to live with Mary and Henry after the death of his mother. (A.D. Vaughn Collection)

for work at the time, but the lure of a woman had clouded his mind. Pop and Grace became friendly, and soon enough, he sired a child by Grace. They named their daughter Rose Nelson. Back then, a man would not acknowledge a child born out of wedlock. He might send the mother some money to help care for the child, but that was not guaranteed. Many fatherless children received public assistance from the state government (Garfinkel, 1988). Rose's existence was kept a secret, and Pop was not revealed until after my mother's passing.

Pop continued to travel to Columbia, SC (Lexington County), where he met my mother, Ella Lloyd. Mama was a native of Lexington, South Carolina, and taught at a Colored

82

school. She had a family of eleven—three sisters and eight brothers. Pop was Mama's second husband. I don't recall what

Ella Lloyd was a teacher in a segregated school, expert seamstress, and homemaker. (A.D. Vaughn Collection)

happened to Mama's first husband, and we didn't really talk about him. Pop courted Mom for some time, and she played hard to get. Eventually, Pop asked Mama's dad, John Lucious, for her hand in marriage, and he said yes. In my day, that is just the way folks got engaged. After they were married, Mama continued to teach, and Pop found work at the local mill. Mama and Pop were on their way to building a decent life for themselves. They had a place to live in a community of people they knew.

My mom had her first child in 1909—Pompie II, named after my paternal grandfather. Little Pompie died shortly after birth, and I think Mama held that pain within her for many years to come. There were very few hospitals for Colored families back then, and lots of Black babies died in our community (Bhatia, Krieger, & Subramanian, 2019). When Mom got pregnant with me, she went to stay near Aunt Jennie. My mother's sister, Jennie, was the midwife for the county. She took care of Black and white babies and was very popular. So, of course, Aunt Jennie helped deliver me. Including me, Mom and Pop had seven children: Pompie II (1909-1909), John (1913-1983), Phoebe (1915-1986), Rachel (1918-1920), Nathaniel (1920-1979) and Elenora (1922-2008).

Arthur Vaughn

We classified Rachel as a doll. She got her light-skinned color from Mama and had Pop's stringy hair. Even though Mama was light-skinned, Pop always referred to his mother when it came to our color. Grandma Phoebe Dawkins-Hill was also of fair skin, according to him. From the photos I've seen of Grandma Phoebe, she had hair piled on top of her head and high cheekbones with the features of someone of Native American descent. Pop was a little color-struck. I think the colorism Pop displayed was a holdover from enslavement, where lighter-skinned Blacks were treated more favorably than darker-skinned Blacks (Harvey, Tennial, & Hudson, 2017; Keith & Herring, 1991).

Rachel died before reaching her third birthday. The day my sister died, Mama called our neighbor, Mrs. Mitchell, to come help her. Mrs. Mitchell knew the child was dying but was hesitant to tell Mama. Mama laid Rachel's body out on our sofa as if she was napping. Losing a second child shattered Mama's heart forever.

Mama was not with me—or us, I should say—for very long. My mother, Ella, was a good Southern cook, and everybody talked about her cooking, especially her biscuits and rolls. I think making rolls was something handed down from generation to generation, starting with Katy Dawkins and passed down to me. Aunt Sallie also made pies, and Bertha made cakes. They always exchanged goodies at holiday times. Mama was also a good tailor. She worked in a factory that made men's coats. She made suits for the neighborhood men, also men's coats, and did not use a pattern.

Pop was very jealous of Mama and let it be known that men were not welcome when he wasn't home. He was the supreme boss in the home. Mama was too smart for her own good, though. But I guess she loved her man and did all she could to please him. She was a good-looking woman, as Pop said, and he expressed jealousy because he knew other men wanted to be with her, too. He always said she was his and his to protect and that she would serve no one but him, nor entertain no man when he was not around, no matter who they were. A potential patron must first get his permission to come, a definite hour, and not stay long. Mama's friends, especially those she knew from childhood, dare not call her Ella. Pop demanded that they address her as Mrs. Hill. He would say, "I know I got the best-looking woman from the area. She is mine, and you can't have her. That's Mrs. Hill to you."

After slavery ended, Black families tended to stay close, and if they did move, they took their extended family with them (Mandle, 1992). They could stand on the porch and call one another from a quarter mile across the field, and in a few minutes, they would hear an answer come back. I believe it was the echo of the voice that carried and was able to reach across the field.

Somehow Aunt Bertha and my mother's brother Walter got together, married, and had a family of seven children. Their union was probably a result of how close all the families lived. Uncle Walter was seven years Aunt Bertha's senior, which wasn't uncommon during this time. One day, I ventured out to go see Aunt Bertha. I was going through the garden path when I came within a foot or two of a snake lying across the path ahead. No way was I going to turn back now. I screamed for my dear life! Someone came to my rescue and chided me because the one ahead of me was dead.

Pop's sister, Mary Hill, Mama's sister, Sallie Lloyd, and her brother, Walter Lloyd, lived a country call from each other.

Arthur Vaughn

Ella Lloyd with her siblings,
Walter Lloyd and Sally Lloyd
(A.D. Vaughn Collection)

Uncle Henry was the last of my Aunt Mary's three husbands. She had conceived from her previous marriages but had no success carrying a baby full term. I believe Aunt Mary was feeling sadness, regret, and self-doubt about not being able to raise any of her own children since each of her children was stillborn. I often wondered if Aunt Mary was overwhelmed by despair after each of her children passed away.

Uncle Henry was the eldest of Pop's family, and Aunt Bertha was their youngest. In addition to Aunt Mary being a surrogate mother to Pop, she filled the same role for her husband's sister, Bertha. As fate would have it, Bertha Cook would marry my mother's brother, Walter Lloyd. She had children, not from Uncle Henry but from previous marriages.

Aunt Mary's husband, Uncle Henry, adored children. He came to pick me up every weekend. So, I spent the weekends with them. My only condition was that Aunt Mary make me an apple pie, or else I would go home. She was very accommodating. I loved her apple pies. I was treated like a queen at Aunt Mary and Uncle Henry's house. Uncle Henry would not let me out of his sight, and whatever I wanted, I got. I picked the apples that Aunt Mary used to make pastries.

Bliss was short-lived when Pop caught me saying cuss words after coming home from visiting with Aunt Mary and Uncle Henry.

"Ella," he said to Mama, using a stern tone, "don't let Rosa Mae go to Henry's house no more. I know it's my sister's house, too, but I don't care whose feelings it hurts. I won't have my child cursing."

Pop was a strict disciplinarian. No drinking, no smoking, no dancing, and certainly no swearing in *his* house. He did not want his children to acquire bad habits because he entertained church dignitaries in his home and couldn't afford to be embarrassed by us. Even Mama had to get his permission to visit her sister, Sallie, or there would be words.

Uncle Henry was the eldest of five or six children, and his parents had passed on. Aunt Mary took the youngest one, Aunt Bertha, into her home to care for her because she had no parents and depended on Uncle Henry, her eldest brother. When Mary became ill with pneumonia, Bertha waited on her hand and foot. It was 1933 when Aunt Mary passed. Aunt Bertha was very shaken up. She stated Aunt Mary was the only mother she had known and therefore had deep feelings for her.

Living in the Styx

Pop was never a farmer. He worked in a rock quarry and later at a mill. For a time, he worked at the Rudy Roe Sawmill in Styx. In addition to the Hills, other families moved to Styx, migrating into the area. Two such families were the Boozers and the Chestnuts, who my parents knew from our time in Columbia. The employees lived in a camp established for them. The houses were more like shanties or first-class shacks—two or three rooms at the most. Families followed the mill because they would have a place to stay and a job to buy food and clothing. There was a company store for short orders or emergency items, but payday found most workers shopping in Columbia, the nearest city to Styx. The churches were in the city. That's what made it easy to establish a mission by the sawmill.

My maternal grandfather bought acres of land in Styx and divided it among Sallie, Ella (my mother), and Uncle Walter— one acre each. My family knew the pain when Black families were pulled apart during slavery. The anger and confusion of being cut off from the world you knew was something my maternal grandfather remembered and hoped we would never experience. The land he purchased for the family was sandy and not suitable for vegetation. It was most likely near Lake Murray. Aunt Sallie kept the taxes paid until she became sick and disabled. We eventually lost all records of the land and assumed another purchased it for the amount equivalent to the back taxes. I always thought it would be nice for our family to buy land near one another to remain close.

I mentioned earlier that Pop had two brothers and one sister, and each of his brothers had a different father—John Pack and Hence. Pop said Grandma Phoebe struggled to raise two kids after her first husband was gone. The prospect of raising two small children and earning a wage to provide for them was more than a notion. It's always been hard on Black women, but having two extra mouths to feed, she did what she had to do to get by (Gaspar & Hine, 1996; Jacobs, 2022). I have to believe she got involved with John's daddy because he had money and promised to care for her and her kids in exchange for sexual relations. According to cousin Gus Dawkins, Uncle John's father was white and provided support for all of his children born in and out of wedlock. It was illegal in those days for Blacks and whites to marry. I was pleased when I learned Grandma Phoebe eventually married again. I never got to know her second husband, William. After Grandma passed, he wasn't around for Pop and Aunt Mary.

Uncle John worked as a Pullman Porter on the railroad and put himself through school. He eventually graduated with a degree in teaching and became qualified to become a school principal in Brevard, South Carolina. Most public schools for Blacks during this time consisted of a two-room log cabin (Anderson, 2010; Tindall, 2021). The two-room, two-teacher log-cabin school was later exchanged with Frank Jenkins for land on West Main Street, where a four-room school was built around 1910. In 1938, the Transylvania County Schools insurance analysis listed the school as a wood frame building with a metal roof and having 4,300 square feet.

Uncle John met and married a fellow teacher, Jessie Dennis. As the story goes, she was a wonderful housekeeper. According to him, she was somewhat senile and could sometimes be hard to get along with. They eventually moved to Styx and built a six-room house just off the highway down an embankment. It was a corner property and close to the airport. They had fruit trees and nice shrubbery on the land. Later on, Jessie became ill and had a breast removed.

During our days in Styx, some revivalists traveled from city to city and state to state. Rev. Mrs. Chiles and her husband came to town and conducted revival meetings. I believe it was a tent meeting where Mama and Pop got saved. After accepting Christ, Pop later acknowledged a call to the ministry. It was about this time I had my first encounter with death.

A man passed our house carrying a wagon with a body in it. It was dressed but not covered or embalmed. If I remember correctly, it was Beulah Chestnut's funeral, the twin sister of Adam Chestnut. The sight was undeniable. 'Twas Beulah Chestnut's funeral made me and my cousin Oscar "Buster" Boozer want to have our own funeral. We were always mimicking someone, especially the preacher. We had no other way to have a funeral but to kill a cat, funeralize it, and dig a hole to bury it. Don't ask me whose idea this was, but most likely, it was mine. So, we did just that, and now I can say I've preached at a funeral.

My school years began when I was about four years old. My

cousin Maggie used to swing by the house and pick me up for school. She took me to an Episcopal Church School in Styx, South Carolina, in present-day Lexington County. Maggie thought I was so cute and would carry me everywhere with her.

Most schools were in a church in those days, and the Episcopal church took a special interest in the education of Colored folk. The school taught us to dance, which I considered a simple exercise. But because dancing was classified as a nonspiritual activity, it was wrong in Pop's eyes, and he almost killed me when he saw me dancing in the kitchen one day. He knocked me out of the back door and down a flight of steps. Screaming, Mama threw her hands up and ran down the stairs behind me, afraid I was seriously injured. She must have thought the worst. She and Pop had words over the incident, and it almost caused a separation. Pop said he would do it again if he caught me dancing.

My relationship with Pop started to change after that day. Pop was supposed to be my protector and shield me from the dangers of the world. However, after he struck me, I began to think I not only had to worry about the dangers in the world but fear my father's temper, as well.

Hearing Pop's stories about how the law treated us helped me understand some of his behavior. I believe Pop's form of corporal punishment towards me and my siblings was out of fear. As I got older, I understood that he feared a white mob or the police might do even worse to us or even kill us if we got out of line. We knew from Pop's stories that life for Blacks in the South was difficult back then.

Arthur Vaughn

April Fool

We later moved from Styx to Pelion, South Carolina, a small town near the railroad. A Black family lived on one side of us, and a white family on the other. The Black family was the McGregors, if I remember correctly. The children were our age, and we became friends. We also lived across the road from a white family.

One day, Mama had to go to town. Before leaving, she instructed me, "Don't open the door for anyone."

I promised her that I would not and that I would take care of my baby sister, Phoebe Hill. You might have already noticed that Phoebe was one of our family names passed down from generation to generation.

Lo and behold, the white girl comes from across the field, knocking to come in. I told her that she would have to wait until Mama came home. She kept annoying me, but I held out.

Finally, she knocked and said, "Here comes your mother." When I opened the door, she yelled, "April fool," came inside, and would not leave.

Mama came home, found her in the house, and gave me one good shellacking. No chance I could explain to her what this white child had done to trick me. She did not want anyone in her house because she was concerned about our safety. That was the first and only time my mother whipped me, but I'll never forget it.

The Great Migration

Another Country

I don't know how Pop had the gall to leave Mama and us children in South Carolina and move to Philadelphia, but he did. We were part of what is known as the Great Migration when six million Blacks moved from the Southern states to the Northeastern, Midwestern, and Western portions of the United States (Baharian, Barakatt, Gignoux, Shringarpure, Errington, Blot, & Gravel, 2016; Derenoncourt, 2022). Mama picked cotton to help support us while waiting for Pop to send for us. We joined him in Philadelphia in 1915. Pop was employed by the powder plant in Kensington, mixing aluminum powder and various colored pigments primarily used in paints and explosives. When he got his first paycheck, he came to get us so we could join him in the

Rev. Benjamin Franklin Hill, born in 1883, was responsible for the Hill families move from the rural south to the industrial north as a part of the Great Migration. (A.D. Vaughn Collection)

North. He boasted that it only took him a few weeks to send for his family. He could not stand to be separated from his family, and it seems he could not do without Mama.

We stayed on Fitzwater Street when we arrived, all in one room. Negro folk settled around Lombard Street and a street named South Street. When we moved up north, we found that folks who were called Colored in the South were now being called Negro (Smith, 1992).

Phoebe was a babe in arms when we came to Philadelphia. John was a knee baby, and I was the babysitter. John was sickly, and lots of attention and prayers went up for him. The influenza was raging in those days, and everybody was doing everything they could to keep from getting it. We thought it was the flu, but the doctor said that wasn't it. They did not know what was wrong with him. The doctor kept coming but never really diagnosed John's case. Mama was very upset, praying and crying for God to have mercy on John and cure him. He was her only son at that time. Mama had locked herself in the bathroom to be alone. When I pushed the bathroom door open, I caught her washed in tears and praying for John's recovery.

Her prayers were answered that Christmas morning. John woke up, saw the toys around the heater, and immediately got out of bed. We ended up having an enjoyable Christmas. He was not sick anymore for many years—at least not physically. However, the high fever must have affected him because shortly after he was enrolled at school, he had to be transferred to a special school for slower children.

In 1920, when I was nine, we moved to N. Franklin Street. We lived on the second floor in an apartment with two large rooms (Thorndale & Dollarhide, 1987). Pop insisted that Mama train me early to keep house and do all the grown-up chores. He even brought home a toy iron or two for me. He must have had a premonition that Mama would not be around very long.

We had gas for lights, cooking, and hot water. The chandeliers were gas, with beautiful globes that covered the light to give off a softer glow. We had a pot-bellied stove in the room for heat, even though the house had a central heating unit. Those things (a central heating unit, a bathroom, and a gas-lit chandelier) were new to us.

I started trying to cook when we moved to Philadelphia. I used a Karo syrup can as a pot. Mama forbade me to do so, but I would do so anyway. I got caught when I made the mistake of sealing the can and putting it on the stove to cook. When the insides started to boil, the top flew off and just missed my forehead. Pop gave me a good spanking because Mama told on me. She did not beat us. Pop handed out the discipline, and because of that, we all feared him.

That Christmas, Santa paid us a visit. We got lots of toys, including cut-out paper dolls, houses, farm scenes, and a toy hand iron. My cousin Buster was a devilish child. He wanted his, yours, and everybody else's toys.

One day, Mama and Aunt Sallie went shopping, and I was to tend to the babies and stay in our quarters till Mama got back. My cousin Buster (Oscar) came up the stairs to our quarters and saw me playing with the toy iron I received for Christmas. Buster was jealous. We quarreled over the hot iron. He got so mad that he snatched up the iron and slammed it down on my left hand. Screaming, I took a freshly heated iron from the heater for revenge. I cried as I chased him to the top floor. If our other cousin had not been home, I would have branded him on the back of the head. He outran me, and our cousin opened the door before I got there and protected him.

Arthur Vaughn

When Pop got home that evening and saw his baby with a burnt hand, swollen and full of water, he wanted to beat Buster, but he didn't. This caused a separation of the two families. Buster's father was a man of few words. Buster only got a scolding—no other punishment. The scar from that burn remains with me to this day. It's not as noticeable as years ago, but it was a horrible scar at the time.

Let's go back a bit and not get too far ahead of my story. I must have been about four years old when Pop brought us to Philadelphia. We were upstairs but had privacy. We used a potbelly stove for heat. It was better than what we had down south. I remember we made ash cakes. Ash cakes are made up of flour/cornmeal, water, baking powder, and salt. After mixing them together, we would make a small pancake and place it on the white ash from a fire. We made sure the fire was hot in the fireplace, swept away all the unwanted dirt and dust from the fire hearth, and poured the batter on the hearth close to the fire. The heat would dry out the batter, then we heaped hot ashes on top of the dough and let it bake. Pop talked about his ash cakes, cornbread, and biscuits. The biscuits were a Sunday meal. We could not afford anything better.

We occupied the two upstairs floors above a hand laundry owned by a Chinese man named Charlie. We had to pass through an alley to a back door that gave us entry to the upper floors. It was also a back entrance to Charlie's Laundry, and we had to be particular about who came in. We would make fun of Mr. Charlie, and he pretended to chase us out of the alley. When the laundry was closed in the evenings and on Sundays, we played jacks on the stoop.

During my lifetime, I witnessed sugar costing $0.05 per pound, three pounds of cornmeal for $0.10, and lard for $0.05

per pound. There was no such thing as a loaf of bread until around 1920. Then we bought bread at a special store. Mama placed an order for bread. It was a weekend sale—no bread before or after then. A loaf of bread was a novelty. Charles Freihofer Baking Company bread was our favorite. 'Twas a long loaf resembling the kind used today for a foot-long sandwich.

I consider Philadelphia, Pennsylvania, my hometown. After us, Mama's sister, brother, mother, and many cousins established themselves there. Because it was deserted, there was really no reason to return to our birthplace.

Arthur Vaughn

The Fire-Baptized Holiness Church

Pop was the first of the men who left South Carolina, but soon after, Uncle Arthur, the Boozers, and the Chestnuts joined us in Philadelphia. Naturally, church was on all our minds after finding a place to stay. Pop would not work on Sundays; church was Pop's middle name. So, we found our way to a storefront church of the same denomination we had attended in South Carolina: Pentecostal.

The Fire-Baptized Holiness Association of Greenville, South Carolina, was founded by William Edward Fuller Sr. in 1898 and emphasized direct personal experience of God through baptism with the Holy Spirit. The Fire-Baptized Holiness Church where we worshiped was struggling to grow. The church didn't have a permanent place to meet. We were renters, and as the church grew, we got larger quarters.

Like Pop, Mama was also a preacher, but I only remember her preaching at platform services. She must have been pregnant or babysitting. Otherwise, she might have been called on other times. Our denomination was not too keen on women evangelizing, but the women outsmarted the bishop. They started their own church and would not report to the Fire-Baptized Church Convention nor allow their church to enroll at the convocation. Bishop relented against the pressure and ended up appointing women to pastor and other positions.

One of the women was Mother Pinkard, a stern and well-educated person. She was also very loving. She took more interest in young people than any other person. She established classes for the girls and taught them about personal life. We learned that keeping house for a husband was more than feeding him. It also involved cleaning the house, doing the laundry, and caring for the children. The girls had to demonstrate their housekeeping ability. The classes were held on Sunday evenings at 6:00 p.m. for one hour. We were also lectured about our bodies. During my church life with the Holiness Church in Philadelphia, I served as secretary of the young people's department and delegate to the convention.

We attended the same school at 5th and Race Street in Philadelphia with our cousins, the Chestnuts and Boozers. The Chestnuts attended Mother Bethel A.M.E. Church, widely recognized as the nation's first Black denomination. Mother Bethel was founded in 1787 by Rev. Richard Allen and rests upon the oldest parcel of land in the United States, continuously owned by African Americans. The Boozers and Hills attended St. Peter Fireside Baptist Holiness Church on 7th and Lombard. The part of the family still residing in Philadelphia continues to attend the same churches.

Arthur Vaughn

Makes Me Wanna Holler

Our one-room home had a potbellied heater and a beautiful gas chandelier that we did not use for fear of the gas and because we didn't know how to keep them in good working order. It was here where Pop would share stories about our ancestors after Sunday dinner. We used kerosene lamps and burned coal for heat.

Speaking of lights, Philadelphia was served by a lamplighter who came along just before dusk to light the lamps. By this time, horse-drawn streetcars had been replaced by electric trolley cars. They would clang, clang, clang up and down the street with a conductor on board. While we were playing one evening, a neighbor's child ran to get her ball to keep the trolley from crushing it; she was crushed instead. The motorman did not see her, but the cries of those on the street attracted his attention. Nothing could bring her back; there was no use in trying to revive her. She was the child of our white neighbors, who we lived by before moving to a newer home. Not only did I witness this tragic incident, but some boys playing in a vacant lot on

Wood and Franklin Street saw it, too.

We were told not to go to the lot to play, but now and then, some of us would go. The fun for most who played there was jumping through the fire. They would build a fire from trash accumulated in the lot, and when the fire became roaring hot, they would jump through it. One of the neighbor's children jumped through and caught fire. The flame spread across his clothing in an instant. His screams aroused everyone nearby. Some men brought him home. It was dreadful to see how burnt he was, and his cries were horrifying. They called the police as there was no ambulance service at that time. They did everything they could for him, but he passed away shortly after he arrived at the hospital. Both the children who died during this time were white.

It was an interesting time in the North back then. We lived in an integrated neighborhood and attended integrated schools but went to segregated churches. When we lived in the South, neighborhoods, schools, and churches were all segregated (Ollie, 1988).

Arthur Vaughn

Dear Brother John

My brother John liked to shoot marbles in the same vacant lot on the corner of Wood and Franklin Street. He was a good shooter. He knew Pop did not approve and would always tell Pop he was not shooting marbles. However, his dirty pants legs would tell on him. That boy couldn't stay off his knees for the life of him. Like my dancing, Pop did not consider shooting marbles a holy activity. Shooting marbles was more aligned with street life than the church.

One day, Pop walked up on him in the act. He almost murdered John. He beat him so badly that I cried along with him. He beat him mercilessly until he said, "Please, Sir Papa" several times until Pop finally let him go. Pop's response was, "You should have said that the first time instead of yelling for the cops to hear you. I'll beat you and the cops."

I hated it when Pop would beat us. More than anything, Pop's beatings did more to diminish my love for him. The physical pain would pass, but the emotional hurt never went away.

My brother John was the sickly one from the time we arrived in Philadelphia and never made the trip to the New York area. The doctors could not diagnose John's illness. He saw our Christmas toys, got out of a sick bed, and did not get sick again until later in life. He was not one to learn fast and attended a special school. Finally, he started doing unordinary things, and they put him in an insane asylum. We neglected him for years because we were ashamed of him. The hospital stated he had been on the dismissal list for years; they thought his family was all dead.

Since he could not be released to anyone out of state, he was placed in a foster home, which became his final resting place. I would say he died of a broken heart. The last time I saw him, he wanted to be with one of us, mainly Pop. When Pop was told he died, he cried like a baby. Tears still come to my eyes when I think about it. They did not give us a cause of death, so they gave him a pauper's burial. When I look back at how we treated my brother, I am more ashamed of my behavior than I was ever ashamed of him. Even though Pop never went to check on him, I could have. I could have brought my brother home. I carried this guilt for many, many years.

Later, my son, Oscar, suffered from mental health challenges. No matter how bad it got, we never allowed him to be admitted to a facility like we did with my brother John. I loved my son and did not abandon him like we did with my brother John.

Arthur Vaughn

A Grandmother's Love

My maternal grandmother Rosena (Davis) Lloyd had three husbands—Jack Luscious, Tom Cole, and Henry Lloyd. She carried the name Lloyd until her death. I remember my maternal grandmother very well.

I was Grandma Rosena's favorite. Pop and her did not get along like they should have because she loved to spoil me, and Pop could not take it. He forbade her to coddle me. He told her that when she's sleeping in her grave, he would still be around. Pop insisted I do as he said or else. We had to move down the street to keep the peace between the two.

One day, I saw Grandma Rosena gasping for breath. She passed away in front of me. I cried uncontrollably when she died. The loss I felt in that moment isn't something I can put into words, but I felt it in my soul. I was about nine or ten years old at the time. Mama and Aunt Sallie accompanied Grandma Rosena's body to Lexington, South Carolina, for the burial. They took the younger children with them and left my cousins Oscar, Henry, and me in Philadelphia.

Oscar and Henry stayed at our house, where Pop was the boss. I was the only one of Mama's children left at home. The other children did not have to have a ticket to travel because they fell under the age of passengers that had to pay. Those few days––not more than two weeks—were miserable for Oscar and Henry. They could not do as they wanted. They were under Pop's strict supervision and knew he did not mind using his belt. To bed at noon, no excuses. After all was said and done, we were thrilled when Mama and Aunt Sallie returned home.

Arthur Vaughn

The Trip to Jewtown

During the period when masses of Black Americans were migrating from the deep south to northern cities, we also found European Jewish immigrants moving to the northeast United States in mass (Meyers, 1998; Baharian, Barakatt, M, Gignoux, Shringarpure, Errington Blot, & Gravel, 2016). Philadelphia, Pennsylvania, was one city that found large numbers of Italians, Hungarians, Rumanians, and Jewish residents (Meyers, 1998). Heilwood was a town where mining dominated and manual labor was found in abundance. North Heilwood was where many of the poor Yiddish-speaking families lived and worked. New to this community where southern blacks found themselves, Fifth Street to the Delaware River and south of Lombard Street. However, many of the businesses in the community were owned by these hardworking Jewish residents (Meyers, 1998).

Pop was almost ten years the senior of Uncle John Sator. He made sure Uncle John went to school, but Uncle John wanted more education. So, he started work early. Uncle John made New York City his headquarters. He ran the Pullman Porter on the railroad from NYC to Florida. I remember when he showed me the first dollar tip he made. He framed it. Uncle John made more money from the tips he received than he did from his actual salary.

When he had time off, he would come to see us in Philadelphia. He saved his pennies for us children. He loved to throw them up in the air and watch us scramble for them. He wanted to do a little more, so he asked Pop to let him buy me a pair of shoes. It was the trip of my life to go downtown to Snellenberg's, a high-class shoe store, to get a pair of shoes. Uncle John took us to Jew Town in Pine Township, where things were up for grabs (Tabak, 1990). There he bought us clothes and shoes. Having never been to an actual shoe store before, I did not know how to get my foot sized. I couldn't tell the difference between tight and too small. New shoes are snug, but I thought they were all too small and wound up with a pair of shoes much too big for me. Uncle

MR. JOHN PULASKI SARTOR

JULY 20, 1973   4 P. M.

MT. OLIVE C.M.E. CHURCH

LEXINGTON, S. C.

REV. B. B. BOOZER, PASTOR

REV. ABRAHAM H. PRINCE, OFFICIATING

John Stator, Jr., was the son of Phoebe Dawkins and John Stator, Sr. He is the younger brother of Mary (Hill) Cook, Benjamin Franklin Hill, and William "Hence" Ruth (A.D. Vaughn Collection)

John still paid for them, though, and I was thrilled to have my first pair of brand-new shoes. I was so happy that I wore them until my feet nearly busted out the front of them. My Uncle John Sator died in 1973.

The War to End All Wars

The Great War had started just before we migrated north. The men in the community were being drafted—all except the Blacks. President Woodrow Wilson declared a "lily White War," which meant no Black GIs (Blumenthal, 1963; O'Reilly, 1997). Wilson was a child of Georgia born just before the start of the Civil War and lived through reconstruction. These experiences were said to shape President Wilson's view and attitude toward Blacks (Blumenthal, 1963). The white women put up a squawk about his all-white war, saying, "Who will be here for our daughters to marry if our boys are killed at war?" The president later adhered to their cry by soliciting and sending ill-trained Black men overseas.

Thousands of Blacks during World War I were sent to France (Keene, 2002; Roberts, 2014). There was a certain bridge they were to cross to arrive at their place of action. The officers knew the bridge was wired with landmines, but to the satisfaction of "White America," the Black troops were ordered to cross. Thousands of Black boys were killed (Roberts, 2014).

During this time, America and her allies were losing the battle, and the order came from the White House to recruit men eighteen to forty-five years old (Kornweibel, 2002). This draft included my father, and he didn't know what to do. However, he decided to play on the sympathy of the precinct captain.

The police department or precincts oversaw the recruits. All eligible men had to register with their district police department. Because Pop was not forty-five years old when the order came down, he was called to report for duty. When the date for him to appear arrived, he had Mama dress us all in our Sunday best. Mama looked good, too. Pop, in his clergy garb, went to face the captain. He would not rely on any other way of convincing the captain but in person. We stood hands joined before the captain, and Pop began to explain the hardship it would put on the family without him in the home, him being the only breadwinner. Mama could not work with such a large family to take care of. There was me, Phoebe, John, and, at the time, Mama was pregnant with Rachel, who would be the first of their children born in the north. The captain was respectful of Pop's clergy attire, and Pop was ever so humble, saying, "Yes, sir," while bowing. The captain stamped his papers and banged his gavel to defer the case for family reasons and because Pop was employed in an industry essential to the war effort: the powder plant where he made ammunition.

When peace was declared in 1918, I was still at school. Sirens, horns, whistles, and all kinds of noisemakers were used to celebrate—even pots, pans, and drums. It was supposed to be a happy day.

Seeing Into Tomorrow

Paxon School was my first school in Philadelphia. We could bring in money once a week for school lunch or to buy crackers and soup during our break time. The teachers collected the money and credited it to us. Mama gave me money to give to the teacher every week. One week, the teacher swore I did not give her the money for a snack. Angry, Mama ended up siding with my teacher, supposing I had spent the money on candy or chewing gum. From that day forward, Mama brought the money to class herself.

We soon moved again from that neighborhood. Popular Street was Black folks' heaven. There was a vegetable market for two or three blocks. From 9th Street to 12th Street, there were Saturday night parties every weekend. Unfortunately, there were shootings and knifings every weekend, too. Finding a body or two lying in the gutter early Sunday morning was ordinary.

Pop made sure to make friends with each of our teachers. He regularly visited our schools, especially while we attended Northeast Manual Training School on 8th Street and Lehigh

Avenue in Philadelphia (Ash, 1909; Neville, 1927). Manual Training schools were just as their names suggested. They were schools designed to prepare students—especially Negro students—for jobs in bricklaying, carpentry, painting, plumbing, sheet metal working, and other industries needed during the industrial age (Ash, 1909; Neville, 1927).

All the students knew Pop. So did the principal, Mr. Riger. Ms. Elsie, the office clerk, was very accommodating. If Mr. Riger was not in, she allowed Pop to wait in the office. We all had Ms. Julia (1st grade) and Ms. Godfrey (2nd grade). Those two became good friends with Pop to the point that Ms. Godfrey often our home. Pop being a minister attracted her; she was a Lutheran. They discussed matters in the Bible and enjoyed each other's company. Ms. Martha was our 4th-grade teacher, and we had Ms. Cohill in the 5th grade. The pretzel lady was a good old-fashioned woman. She was Jewish and did not work or come to sell her pretzels on Jewish holidays.

Before I attended Junior High School, I attended 6th grade at Northeast Grammar School. Many primary and secondary schools for Negro children were not designed for any form of higher learning that could liken to college enrollment. Schools were intended to retain Negros who were used to agricultural work in the south to work at factories in the northern states (Greenwood, 2010).

Beloved

In Philadelphia, it was customary for three or four families to live together in one big house and pool their resources. However, Pop always wanted to be his own man and not knuckle under anyone, especially his in-laws and particularly my maternal grandmother. Grandma Rosena was strong-willed and challenged my father's views as he was the head of our household. The conflict between Pop and Grandma Rosena also created friction between him and Mama.

We moved to our own place down the street on Franklin Street to keep the peace. Things were a lot better for the family for a time after we moved. Uncle Henry and Pop's sister, Aunt Mary, lived above us, but I did not see Grandma Rosena as much. I really missed her.

A few years after moving to our new home, Mama fell ill. I sat by my mother's bed, praying God would heal her. I was twelve years old and did not know why she was being taken away from us. I did not know what I would do without the woman I had depended on all my life. Mama was everything to me. As I watched her take her last breath, hurt and pain rushed over me like a tidal wave. It was December 7, 1923, and my mama was gone.

Mama had been an ordained gospel minister and was entitled to funeral honors. It was the ruling Elder C.A. Mills' duty to preach her funeral. According to Pop, he made some embarrassing remarks during the funeral service. My father never forgave Elder Mills, and their relationship from then on was very cold toward one another. Because Elder Mills had the bishop's ear, Pop never got anywhere in the church and was never given a lucrative pastoral assignment.

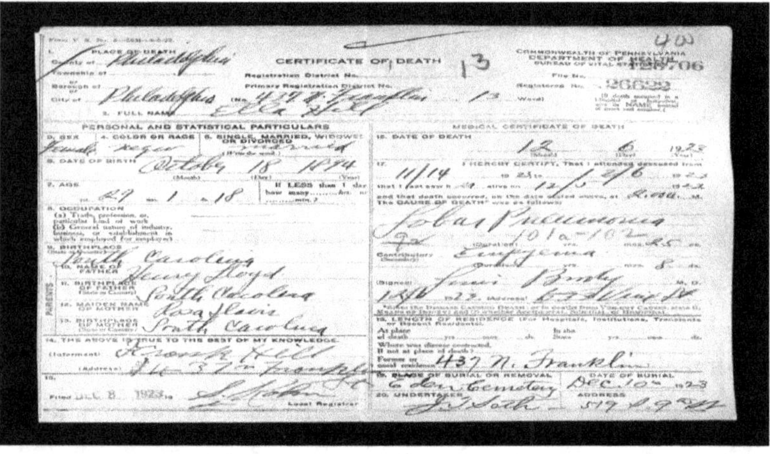

Ella (Lloyd) Hill Death Certificate. Ella was an ordained minister in a time when there were few women who openly preached. She passed away six years before the Great Depression. (A.D. Vaughn Collection).

Nobody Knows My Name

When Mama passed, everything she did for the family—the washing, ironing, cooking, cleaning, and other household chores—became my burden. I cried myself to sleep each night because I wanted my mother. She would show up in my dreams, and when I awoke, she was gone. She visited me in my dreams for many years.

Shortly after my mother died, my illegitimate half-sister, Rose Nelson, came to stay with the Chestnut family in Philadelphia. Pop and her mother, Grace, had a sexual encounter on a train back in his hobo days that resulted in Rose's birth, but Pop never had a relationship with Rose. In those days, when a man had a child with a woman he was not married to, the child was not acknowledged by the father or his family (Garfinkel, 1988). However, men with a conscience would send money to help support the child.

Years after Rose's birth, Grace married into the Chestnut family, which made things even more complicated. Mama's sister, Dellie, married into the Chestnut family, making Rose her niece by marriage. Further complicating matters, Aunt Sallie (Lloyd) Boozer lived a few doors from her sister, Aunt Dellie (Lloyd) Chestnut. Pop regularly visited Aunt Sallie's house so he could see Rose Nelson a few doors down at Aunt Dellie's home. Initially, he did not speak to Rose. He only wanted to lay eyes on his long-lost daughter.

Rose's mother raised her to believe the man she married was her father, not Pop. Her mother did not realize Pop was brazen enough to tell her that he was her father, that she was the result of the encounter in the freight car. He took courage by purchasing flowers and another item—which I no longer recall––and went to introduce himself to Rose, who was now an adult. Naturally, she couldn't believe what she was hearing. She asked the relatives she was staying with who this old man was that was paying her so much attention and was amazed to learn he had been telling the truth. When Rose's mother, Grace, heard what my father had done, she pitched a fit. She did not think any such thing would happen.

My mother, Ella Lloyd, had passed. So, when Rose came to Philly, there was no fuss over my father's capers or acknowledgment of Rose. Rose and the Boozer family became great friends. We, the Hills, however, did not become friendly with her. I never understood my father's need to reach out to this woman. We lived without knowing she existed for years until he suddenly introduced her into our lives. Adding insult to injury, she and I had the same name, which angered me to no end.

Eminent Domain

Shortly after World War I ended, the Delaware River Bridge was in the making (Dale, 2003). They informed us that our school would be torn down to make room for this project. At the time, it was to be the longest suspension bridge ever made (Buonopane & Billington, 1993). The authorities confiscated our school, and we were transferred to a newly-built school at Fairmont Avenue and Eighth Street. They named it Kearny Junior High School, and Mr. Nevelle was the principal. The novelty of attending this school was that we had a homeroom teacher we reported to each morning and a roster of classes to be at each day. This was new to most of us, but the teacher also swelled our heads by addressing us as Mr. or Miss. She also gave us a pep talk, saying we were no longer babies. We were young adults and were to be treated as such at school and perhaps at home if our parents agreed.

Each class was forty-five minutes. We changed classrooms and teachers, reporting to a class according to our subjects. I think this routine was to get us familiar with what was to come in high school.

After graduating from junior high school, I attended William Penn High School. There were very few Blacks in the school I attended. My cousin Bertha and I were the only Black kids in our classes. I met Thelma Anderson on my way from 6th Street to William Penn. She and I became good friends. She was a decent type of person who I was not afraid to mingle with, and she had stringent parents. Her mother wanted to be acquainted with Pop through our friendship but never did.

I like to sleep in, but Thelma would make sure I woke up to get me going. Bear in mind, I had to freshen up, get dressed, make my bed, see to it that the younger children got dressed and out to school, and start supper. If something had to be boiled for a long time, I could leave it cooking or ask Phoebe or John to stir the pot when they came in from school at 3:30 p.m. My school day started later than theirs. So, I would arrive home at about 5:00 p.m. and Pop shortly after if he was working.

Thelma, Bertha, and I were like triplets. When you saw one, you saw the other two. When it was time for us to attend high school, Thelma and I chose William Penn, which offered academic and business courses. Bertha chose Girls High, which was only academic. Our folks did not relish the idea of their children going to a purely academic high school. Few girls whose parents could afford to send them to college would go there. They were highfalutin and thought they were better than us. In later years, Girls High was very much Black (Neville,1927).

William Penn was famous for their business courses. At that time, I was a high school junior, and very few Blacks were in the schools. The few Blacks chose their class schedules together and made sure to have lunch period and assembly at the same

122

time. Not that the white girls were snooty or nasty. We just wanted it that way. After about two years at William Penn, there was an influx of Blacks there, and it almost became an all-Black school. Phoebe was a part of the influx of Blacks to William Penn. They were called "war babies."

One day while at lunch, I was trying to decide whether to continue going to school or drop out so I could work. Mama was gone, Pop was having a hard time paying the bills, and my younger brothers and sisters needed to be taken care of. I closed my eyes and prayed for guidance. That's when I heard a voice say to me, "Look down at your feet."

I was alone that day. For some reason, Thelma and I were not together. I did as the voice directed me. There was a wad of money at my feet. As I scrambled to pick it up, I looked around to see if anyone saw me. I asked around to see if anyone had lost money, but no claims were made. When school let out, I rushed home to give Pop the money. He was unemployed and had no money, nor was there any food in the house for us to eat. He was very grateful for the cash but was also suspicious. He thought I had "pulled a trick," as they called it, to get the money. However, he did not give it back to me. We ate off that money for a few days.

Arthur Vaughn

Inner City Blues

Years after Mama passed, Pop was engaged to marry a woman who lived next door to us in Philadelphia. We could go from our backyard to her backyard and visit. She and Pop had met previously but never got to know each other. In those days, women who lost husbands usually remarried rather than stay single and suffer the disgraceful whispers because they were seen too often with the same man or the man paid too many visits. It worked out, given the convenient location of the backyards plus the fact that both of their spouses had passed away. She had known Mama, but Pop did not know her husband.

Her name was Beulah Harvey, and she had a daughter named Cynthia, who was younger than me. Cynthia was a streetwise sister and dipped snuff just like her mama. To Pop's benefit, Beulah said she had become saved and sanctified. Personally, I never believed her spiritual revelation. I knew Pop dared not walk into his church on his wedding day with a sinner woman when ninety-nine percent of the women in his church would give anything to be the next Mrs. Hill. Marrying a preacher back then was a big deal and a status symbol.

No matter how many contenders had their eyes on Pop, Beulah would not let go. She had a gigolo in Philadelphia but still wanted Pop. The younger man that she was involved with was living off the earnings and gifts she gave him, and in return, he offered her sexual attention and companionship.

Beulah decided to sell her home in Philadelphia and take an apartment in Brooklyn, New York, until she could find a home suitable for her and Pop. After she arrived in Brooklyn, she met another gigolo. This man's business was prostitution and hustling games on the weekends. He persuaded Beulah to rent an apartment for him in the rear of her apartment and removed some of the wall to make an eight-room flat. The four rear rooms were for games and prostitution. He convinced her that she could be rich and the law would be none the wiser. I suppose this is why Beulah was so willing to take the four extra rooms. I believe her daughter turned some tricks, too, because she always had money.

This "boyfriend" in Brooklyn knew about Pop, but Pop did not know about him. Pop later found out about Beulah's entire situation in Brooklyn and ended his relationship with her. I was glad he did because, as a young woman, I feared being induced into that lifestyle myself.

Arthur Vaughn

In Celebration of
My Spiritual Father

I got saved and sanctified under Rev. G.C. Curry the year after Mama was buried—July 4, 1924. I followed the path my parents had set out for me and was always in church. I was a Sunday school scholar who taught Sunday school. Later, I attended Bible class at Mt. Zion F.B.H.C., where Rev. B.B. Bonner was our teacher. He did not limit the class to preachers. Laypersons were welcome, as well. His adopted daughter, Lillian, was his assistant. She showed us how to take the four New Testament gospels and put Christ's life in chronological order. This is the way we learned. He did not believe in holding service all day and all night. Some people did not like him on that account. They would defy him by coming to church at 9 p.m. on Sunday, which is the time he would be dismissing service.

Boys and Men

Enough about that. I had to grow up earlier than most girls because I had lost my mother and had family responsibilities to manage. With all I had to do, I still found time to pay attention to the young men that came around with my cousin, Oscar. Whenever I was in the company of certain family members, they would make sarcastic remarks about a boyfriend. Several men in my mother's age bracket wanted to get next to me, but when Pop got wind of it, he let it be known that it would be "over his dead body." However, time brings on changes.

One of the men, Robert Boozer, was Aunt Sallie's brother-in-law. Two things: he liked to get liquored up, and he was too old for me. Pop could accept and live with that, though. The bottle did not control him, so to speak. Plus, he was not saved and sanctified, so that's how things stood on that matter.

Robert was careful about how he spent money. He bought a brand-new car, not a second-hand one. I think he paid cash for it. His first venture was to tempt me and impress the old man, I guess. He called on me and asked Pop if he could give me a ride in his new car. In those days, the law was more relaxed about driver tests and licenses for new car owners. Only the vehicle had to be licensed, not the driver.

Robert took me to one of the city's busiest sections, Broad Street and Girard Avenue. When he tried to make a turn to take me back home, as we had gone far enough, we almost had an accident. I was so scared that I refused to allow him to take me riding again. Besides, I was not interested in dating an old man. No way. He had been married, and his wife had passed on.

One day, he stumbled out of his room to call for assistance. He must have leaned over the rail too far and fell to his death. He was drunk on that day, too.

I met a girl at school named Thelma, and we both started working at the Philadelphia Toilet Steam Laundry as mangle feeders. I did not like the work because I had to sort dirty clothes. I found out firsthand with that job how dirty, nasty, and sloppy some people can be. Some bundles were crawling with roaches, some with maggots, and some with bedbugs. We were trained to avoid handling such bundles. We gave them to our boss, who would spray them and sort them himself. I was only fourteen years old but was trying to pass for seventeen. The boss liked my work, and because I was tall, I had the advantage over some of the girls. I was shifted to the shirt department and taught to operate the machines to press shirts. I worked up to pressing 1,000 shirts from 9 a.m.–5 p.m. The wages were $6.50 per week or whatever you could do as a piece worker per week. Thelma and I got along, but the boss favored me more than her.

My time at the Philadelphia Toilet Steam Laundry ended when I admitted to going to school. They wanted no schoolgirls or dropouts working there. So, I went to another laundry where they were in need of press operators. I lied about my age and was hired by Cornell Stream Laundry.

While waiting for the boss to interview me for the job, I noticed Alfred Woodall on the dock, loading laundry onto a big Mac truck for delivery. He said hello and introduced himself. I introduced myself, as well. He later told me that I gave him my address and phone number. To this day, I do not remember doing so. I believe he got my address from a girl named Sadie, who I was assigned to work with.

Before I was given the job, Alfred and I talked to get acquainted. I found out that he knew some of my kinfolk. My first cousin Mary's husband worked at the laundry. He had gone home that night and talked about me to Mary, and from his description and finally my name, Mary told him I was her first cousin.

Having a phone at home was a rare commodity in those days. If you had one, people thought you were rich or somebody special. You had to take messages for the neighbors to use their phone. In fact, the man who rented us the house was the owner, but we were allowed to use his phone, and we compensated for it by taking his messages. Alfred had been by my house and heard the phone ring. He asked to use the phone and took the number, he said. But what had happened was he had overheard my conversation with Sadie and got the number as I gave it to her.

One day, I had this dream about a lottery number. Someone wanted me to give them the number because I did not play the lottery. I told her my number, and she ended up winning. My fame grew. I began getting annoyed by people asking me to give them numbers. Even family and friends had heard and were after me for a number. They all promised to share the winnings if they got lucky.

Privileges

Even though I changed jobs, Thelma and I remained close. Thelma was much more streetwise than me. She ventured out early, although her immediate family was only her brother, mother, and father. She had oodles of 1st cousins. In her age group, she had a cousin, Annie. She and Annie shared experiences and other personal matters. She always had something to tell me that Annie said or had done over the weekend. Annie had a boyfriend named Richard. He was the type that roamed from girl to girl. So, when Richard met Thelma, he seduced her, of course. I could see through all of Richard's tactics, but he had Thelma fooled.

He supposedly fell head over heels in love with Thelma but never quite gave up on Annie. Thelma gave him privileges. She thought having a sexual relationship would keep him from Annie, but it did not. He professed undying love for Thelma and made her believe him. She was like a sick kitten. He was all she would talk about, not to mention his sex habits. She admitted that even though Richard would go to bed with Annie now and then, it was alright because she was so much in love with him. She proposed they marry because she was ruining her health by getting rid of babies and had about exhausted her bank account paying for back-alley procedures. She kept the abortions from her mother until they caught up with her and made her deathly sick. Her mother was suspicious but did not believe Thelma would do such a thing. Although I was no saint, I cried when I thought of what my friend was going through. I believed abortion and premarital sex were both against God's commandments, but in the moment, I just wanted my friend to be alright.

To my and her mother's surprise, Thelma later eloped with Richard, but he never gave up Annie. My good friend Thelma was experiencing low self-esteem and settled for sharing him. When I would hear her be critical of herself, I knew there was little I could do but support her in whatever way I could. I watched as she exhausted her bank account by buying a house and furniture to make a nice home for them.

Richard still did not give up Annie, though. He finally told Thelma that he did not love her. It was Annie he loved. Thelma blamed herself for Richard's behavior and was ready to commit suicide. Thelma's health began to fail; her body had suffered greatly from having so many abortions. The doctors told her she would not get well.

She bought the house using the money she had saved to care for her mother in old age. Upon Thelma's death, Richard took over the house, withdrew all of Thelma's money from the bank, and married Annie. Richard should not have been entitled to anything. He was a man of low character who treated women with little to no respect. Thelma's death was a sad day in her mother's life and mine, too!

Arthur Vaughn

The Song of Solomon

One evening, Rev. Harten of Holy Trinity Baptist Church in Brooklyn, New York, was conducting a revival meeting in Philadelphia. He was a well-known preacher throughout the eastern United States because he preached so many popular sermons and was very expressive when he preached. He climbed the church wall, walked the altar, and crawled around. Pop wanted to see him in action, so he joined me, Sadie, and her friend, Alfred Woodall, to go see Harten preach.

After attending the service, Alfred would not leave me alone. He had moved to Philadelphia from Americus, Georgia, during the Great Depression and found work as a driver with the local laundry company. He would come by my house to discuss Sunday School lessons and presented himself as an officer of the church just to get into the house and talk to me. He would say he called to get my permission, but I did not recall saying yes. He annoyed me when he would come by to talk to Pop because I knew his real reason for being there was to see me.

My brother John used to sit around and listen to him. Alfred always tried to get John's attention because I busied myself in the house and had no time for him. John would tease me about him when he left. Alfred made gestures with his lips, and John mocked him. He would fall asleep, and saliva would drool from his mouth, soiling his jacket and shirt, but he didn't seem to be the least bit embarrassed. Most times, he had no hankie to wipe away the saliva. So, he would use his hand or sleeve. He made a habit of coming by around dinner time, and Pop would offer that he stay and eat, to which Alfred would always reply, "I believe I will."

Alfred D. Woodall Sr.
(A.D. Vaughn Collection)

This galled me to no end, but when I complained to Pop that he was using us to get a free meal, he did not agree. "Let the man eat," Pop would say.

Alfred talked religion and accepted Pop's invitations to go to church, which was next door to where we lived and one flight up. He never left until Pop got tired of talking or had to leave on business. Pop would never leave Alfred or any man in his home if he was not there.

When Alfred asked me to marry him, Pop did not hesitate to tell him yes without my consent. Pop never talked to me or asked me if I wanted to marry the guy or if I was even in love with him. I truly was not ready for marriage. Even if I were to consent to getting married, it wouldn't have been to Alfred Woodall.

Arthur Vaughn

Rosa Mae (Hill) Woodall circa
1950 in Brooklyn, New York
(A.D. Vaughn Collection)

After that exchange, Alfred would drop by the house as usual for a meal. To make conversation, he would ask me who I thought would win baseball's pennant that year. The only thing I knew about baseball was that Alfred liked talking about it. I just named the Brooklyn Dodgers to get him to stop talking. He was in the Phillies' corner and all National League teams.

"Why do you say Brooklyn?" he asked. "Do you have folks in New York?"

"No folks, but I do have friends in Brooklyn," I told him.

Through conversation, I found out I had met most of Alfred's kindred that lived in Brooklyn. He said he had first cousins there and doubted I knew them. He called a few names, and I knew them all.

As I began warming up to the idea of being with this man, we went to Atlantic City for the 4th of July and then again on Labor Day. I still wasn't sure about marriage, but I could not run away because I had no money and no place to hide. So, I decided to pretend marriage to get away from home and all the restrictions and responsibilities that come with family. My younger sister, Nora, and my younger brother, Nate, were still small, but I thought they would get along fine without me.

I grew to love Alfred, and lo and behold, I said "I do" on February 11, 1931, and moved out of the house. I did not know that without my financial contribution, Pop did not have the

134

Rosa Mae (Hill) & Alfred
Woodall circa 1950s
(A.D. Vaughn Collection)

money he needed to pay his rent for the place where he and my siblings lived. Pop would come to see me often and thought I could financially help him somehow.

I had been strapped with children all my life and wanted out. Little did I realize that by getting married, I had put myself in a position to raise a family. But of course, I would be smart and not have babies. Ha! Ha! Ha! I was wrong. They came faster than I could change diapers. Soon, I had my first two children—Alfred, Jr. and then Delores. No matter how much I didn't want to be bothered by little ones, there was no escape for me.

In 1934, our growing family moved from Philadelphia to Brooklyn, New York. The roaring 20s made New York the place to be, but as the Great Depression began, opportunities started to decline. Alfred firmly believed we could make our way in New York. He found work with Bethlehem Steel and the Brooklyn Navy Yard. Mimicking the footsteps of Madame C.J. Walker (The Black Rose), I attended and graduated

As a skilled machinist, Alfred Woodall made parts for American Warships at Bethlehem Steel in Brooklyn, New York. Circa 1940s and 50s (A.D. Vaughn Collection)

Arthur Vaughn

from Robert's Beauty School circa 1940 and earned a beautician's license. With my license in hand, I opened Mae's Beauty Nook when all the Negro women wanted was a shampoo, press, and curl. But things change. When permanents became all the rage, I traded in my hot comb and curling iron for a position with the New York City Social Services Department. Alfred and I made a good life for ourselves and were happy.

Then, in December 1941, the United States entered World War II, and I thought our good life was going to come to an end. While overall unemployment was down, unemployment for Negros—as we were still called—was higher than the country's average (Kersten, 2002). Employment discrimination was prevalent in the growing war-related industries, as was the norm, with upwards of fifty percent of the jobs being reserved for white men (Seidman, 1946; Kersten, 2000). The masses of Blacks that moved from the South found themselves in segregated ghettos with the proliferation of public housing projects after the passage of the 1937 Housing Act (Bloom, 2014; Friedman, 1966).

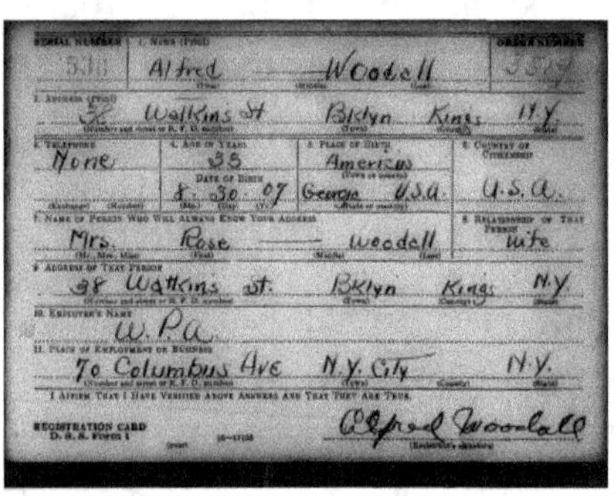

Courtesy Department of Selective Services.

I not only feared Alfred losing his job but also worried he would be drafted. Pop was subject to the draft during the First World War but not selected for service. I did not know what

136

would happen to my husband. President Franklin Roosevelt may not have had the same lily-white military attitude that Woodrow Wilson had during the First World War, but he did believe in segregated units and the limited induction of Negros into the armed service (Kersten, 2002).

Alfred registered for the draft but was not drafted into the service, but he supported the war while working in the Brooklyn Navy Yard. He helped to build some of the United States' mightiest warships (Berner, 1999). We were fortunate. The work Alfred and I were doing allowed us to purchase our home, a brownstone on Union Street in Brooklyn, New York, during a time when Black family incomes were twenty percent of that of whites (Allen & Farley, 1986; Maloney, 1994). This was just as the country was coming out of the Great Depression, and housing prices were a bit

This home at 1429 Union Street in Brooklyn, NY. was the Woodall Family Home. The children of Rosa Mae and Alfred Woodall called this home, as did their grandchildren and many of their great-grandchildren (A.D. Vaughn Collection)

lower than they had been a decade earlier (Nicholas & Scherbina, 2013).

Pop would come to our house on Union Street in Brooklyn because he loved it and thought I was rich. He thought I had money to loan him so he could buy his own place. Pop never felt he could buy a house with the money he made in Philadelphia.

During the rare moment when he had money, he ran into segregation ordinances that prevented Black families from buying homes in certain neighborhoods (Silva, 2009; Woods, 2012).

I learned Pop was now penniless, so he moved into the house with me without my consent. Having my kids, Pop, and others living with Alfred and me was overwhelming. We were not able to help Pop with money, but he was able to save some money while living with us. I love my family, but from raising my siblings while growing up to raising my own kids, I never had a chance to explore what I wanted out of life.

The Wife of His Youth

Pop continued to preach in New Jersey and South Carolina. The years had not been kind to him. As I mentioned, he was never given a lucrative church assignment and struggled to make ends meet. With us out of the house and living our own lives, Pop became more isolated. Then, he met a woman from Anderson, South Carolina, named Corrine Taynum. Corrine was considerably younger than Pop. In fact, she was eight years younger than me. I am not sure what the initial connection was, but Pop was happy, and I assume she was, as well. I imagine her father "gave her away" like mine had done with me when Alfred asked for my hand in marriage. The practice of fathers deciding who their daughters would marry was carried over from slavery and continued through my lifetime (McKittrick, 2006). It felt as if Pop was trying to relive his youth in his old age.

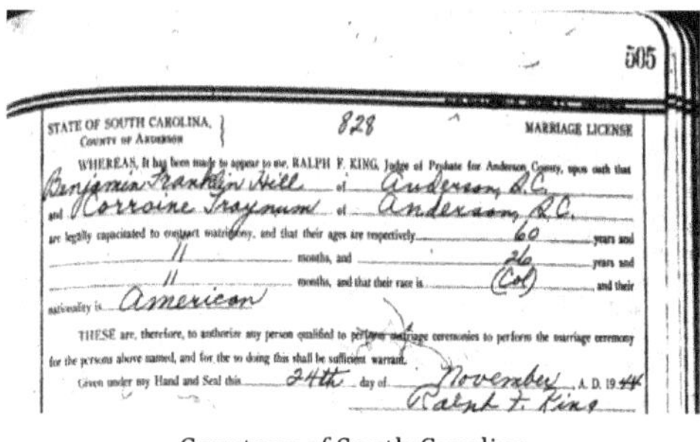

Courtesy of South Carolina
Department of Vital Records

They did not court for long, and on November 25, 1944, Corrine and Pop were married.

My father was sixty years old, and Corrine was twenty-five at the time of their wedding. I had so much going on in my life that I paid little attention to the age difference between Pop and his new wife. I was trying to focus on being a good wife and mother. Alfred and I had five children—Alfred Jr., Delores, Benjamin "Benny," Oscar, and Ella—and I was pregnant with my youngest daughter, Rosa Mae. I had lost a set of twins during childbirth: Gerald and Geraldine. Losing the twins left me feeling like I had lost a limb. My children were lost but still attached to me. They were gone, but the pain was still there.

Pop and Corrine would visit us from time to time, and our kids knew Corrine as the only grandmother they had. My children and younger siblings from my father and Corrine's union grew up like cousins, as my kids were older than Pop's second set of children.

Without a lot of money, Pop and his new family occupied the basement apartment, which was not suitable for his wife and small children. After Corrine and Pop's wedding, the bishop assigned him to Mt. Zion Fireside Baptist Holiness Church in Jersey City, New Jersey. The church Pop led still stands today on Kearny Avenue.

Not long after they were wed, Pop started a new family with his young wife. My sister, Flora May, was born in 1945, followed by Benjamin Jr. in 1948. Pop died in 1951, the same year his youngest son, Ralph, was born. It saddened me that my father never seemed to experience good things in life.

Pop experienced the hardships of bigotry and racism every day in the post-Civil War South. Without the benefit of a mother or father in his life, he tried to be the kind of husband and father he never saw himself. In hopes of prosperity, he moved us north only to find separate and unequal housing, education, and job opportunities (Ollie, 1988). The Negro in America couldn't use the same public facilities as white people, live in many of the same towns, or go to the same schools. He lived out his calling as a man of God and died penniless. However, because of the work he did to help others, his funeral was so big that it could not be held in the sanctuary of his church. My father was memorialized at the Methodist church located about two doors from where he lived in Jersey City, New Jersey.

I learned so many things from the hardships my father experienced—some good and some bad. He was in the first generation of free southern Black people in America. Pop knew what it meant to be Colored and then Negro in America (Martin,1991).

I lived to see the Negro in America experience a new sense of pride during the Civil Rights Movement of the 1950s and 1960s. I was able to "Say It Loud. I'm Black, and I'm Proud." I watched my grandchildren experience a fuller sense of the American Dream as they were members of the first generation in our family to have a college education as a realistic option. My grandchildren refer to themselves as African American (Martin,1991).

As I look down on them from heaven, I watch as my family experiences things that occurred only in my wildest dreams. You see, I passed away on April 15, 2003. In death, I was reunited with my husband, Alfred David Woodall, Sr., and my children, Gerald and Geraldine Woodall, Oscar Charles Woodall, and Delores Woodall-Vaughn. Together, we watch over my living sons, Alfred David, Jr. and Benjamin Franklin; two daughters, Ella and Rosa Mae; my two sisters, Nora Hill-

Arthur Vaughn

Wise and Flora Hill-Long; my brother, Benjamin Franklin Hill, Jr.; my twenty grandchildren and a host of great-grandchildren, nieces, and nephews.

I Sit in the Shade of Trees
I Did Not Plant

I am Arthur David Vaughn, the youngest son of the union of Delores Marie (Woodall) Vaughn and Alfred McKinley Vaughn, Sr. Delores is the daughter of Rosa Mae (Hill) Woodall, who is the eldest daughter of Benjamin Franklin "Pop" Hill, who was the son of

Phoebe Dawkins, who was the daughter of Randle Dawkins, who was the son of Katy Dawkins.

Katy Dawkins was enslaved, spent most of her life in bondage, and never experienced the freedom I sometimes take for granted. Because of Katy, I value my freedom to move as I desire without the threat of the whip or being in bondage.

Randle Dawkins was enslaved, but his mind was free to dream. Even as an enslaved person, Randle was an advocate for those less fortunate than he was. It is because of Randle that I have the ability to use my platform to tell stories and fight for the rights of others.

Phoebe Dawkins was the first in our family to transition from being enslaved to being emancipated under the law.

Arthur Vaughn

Because of Phoebe, I understand my unalienable right to be free from external control and constraint and live as I want to.

Benjamin Franklin Hill chose to relinquish his wicked ways as a child and follow his spiritual call to lead a Christ-centered life no matter how difficult things were for him. It is because of Benjamin that I understand service over self-interest.

My grandmother, Rosa Mae Woodall, was the first in our family to earn a high school diploma. She later went on to further her education and become a licensed beautician. Because of Rosa Mae, I appreciate the value of education and entrepreneurism.

My mother, Delores Marie Vaughn, cared for me through thick and thin. Delores sacrificed her happiness to ensure her children were happy. She never asked me *if* I was going to college but *where* I was going to college. Because of Delores, I know what it is to be loved unconditionally.

Because of Katy, Phoebe, Rosa Mae, and Delores, we know the power of a woman's love can impact a family.

I am Rosa Mae (Hill) Woodall. Each of us has a story. I am no longer here to tell them, but my grandson, Arthur David Vaughn, Ed.D., and my granddaughter, Rosa Mae Dericott, Ed.D., should be proud of their collaboration in the telling of our family's story, *Through My Eyes*.

References

1.   Adamson, C. R. (1983). "Punishment after slavery: Southern state penal systems, 1865-1890". Social Problems, 30(5), 555-569.

2.   Allen, W. R., & Farley, R. (1986). "The shifting social and economic tides of Black America, 1950-1980". Annual review of sociology, 12(1), 277-306.

3.   Amer, M. L. (2005, August). *Black Members of the United States Congress: 1870-2005*. Library of Congress Washington DC Congressional Research Office.

4.   Anderson, J. D. (2010). "The education of Blacks in the South, 1860-1935". Univ of North Carolina Press.

5.   Ash, W. C. (1909). "The Philadelphia Trades School". The ANNALS of the American Academy of Political and Social Science, 33(1), 85-88.

6.   Barker, K. L., Strauss, M. L., Brown, J. K., Blomberg, C. L., & Williams, M. (Eds.). (2020). NIV study bible. Zondervan.

7.   Baharian, S., Barakatt, M., Gignoux, C. R., Shringarpure, S., Errington, J., Blot, W. J., ... & Gravel, S. (2016). "The great migration and African-American genomic diversity". PLoS genetics, 12(5), e1006059.

8.   Barnard, W. D. (1984). *Dixiecrats and Democrats*: Alabama Politics. University of Alabama Press.

9.   Basinger, S. J. (2003). "Regulating Slavery: Deck-Stacking and Credible Commitment in the Fugitive Slave Act of 1850". Journal of Law, Economics, and Organization, 19(2), 307-342.

10. Benton, A. (2016). "What's the matter boss, we sick? A meditation on Ebola's origin stories". Ebola's message: Public health and medicine in the twenty, 85-94.

11. Berner, T. F. (1999). *The Brooklyn Navy Yard*. Arcadia Publishing.

12. Bhatia, A., Krieger, N., & Subramanian, S. V. (2019). *Learning from history about reducing infant mortality: contrasting the centrality of structural interventions to early 20th-century successes in the United States to their neglect in current global initiatives*. The Milbank Quarterly, 97(1), 285-345.

13. Blassingame, J. W. (1965). "The Union Army as an educational institution for Negroes, 1862-1865". The Journal of Negro Education, 34(2), 152-159.

14. Blumenthal, H. (1963). "Woodrow Wilson and the Race Question". The Journal of Negro History, 48(1), 1-21.

15. Blythe, E. K. (2012). "Winter Propagation of Confederate Rose (Hibiscus mutabilis) with Hardwood Cuttings". Proceedings of the International Plant Propagators Society-2012 1014, 151-154.

16. Bonilla-Silva, E. (2004). "From bi-racial to tri-racial: Towards a new system of racial stratification in the USA". Ethnic and racial studies, 27(6), 931-950.

17. Bloom, N. D. (2014). *Public housing that worked: New York in the twentieth century*. University of Pennsylvania Press.

18. Bretz, J. P. (1929). "The Economic Background of the Liberty Party". The American Historical Review, 34(2), 250-264.

19. Brown, R. D., Tager, J., Handlin, O., & O'Connor, T. H. (2015). "Breckinridge, John C. The Early Republic and Antebellum America". An Encyclopedia of Social, Political, Cultural, and Economic History, 158.

20. Bullard, S. (Ed.). (1998). *The Ku Klux Klan: A history of racism & violence*. Diane Publishing.

21. Buonopane, S. G., & Billington, D. P. (1993). "Theory and history of suspension bridge design from 1823 to 1940". Journal of Structural Engineering, 119(3), 954-977.

22. Cauthen, C. E. (2005). *South Carolina Goes to War,*

1860-1865. Univ of South Carolina Press.

23. Dale, F. T. (2003). *Bridges over the Delaware River: a history of crossings*. Rutgers University Press.

24. Daniel, P. (1972). *The shadow of slavery: peonage in the South, 1901-1969*. University of Illinois Press.

25. Derenoncourt, E. (2022). "Can you move to opportunity? Evidence from the Great Migration". American Economic Review, 112(2), 369-408.

26. Drewal, H. J. (2008). "Mami Wata: Arts for water spirits in Africa and its diasporas. African arts", 41(2), 60-83.

27. Eltis, D. (2007). *A brief overview of the Trans-Atlantic Slave Trade. Voyages*: The trans-Atlantic slave trade database, 1700-1810.

28. Finkelman, P. (1997). *Crimes of love, misdemeanors of passion: The regulation of race and sex in the colonial South. The devil's lane: Sex and race in the early south*, 124-38.

29. Foner, E. (2015). *Gateway to freedom: The hidden history of the underground railroad*. WW Norton & Company.

30. Forret, J. (2016). " Deaf & Dumb, Blind, Insane, or Idiotic": The Census, Slaves, and Disability in the Late Antebellum South. The Journal of Southern History, 82(3), 503-548.

31. Franklin, J. H., & Schweninger, L. (2000). *Runaway slaves: Rebels on the plantation*. OUP USA.

32. Friedman, L. M. (1966). *Public housing and the poor: an overview*. Calif. L. Rev., 54, 642.

33. Gallay, A. (Ed.). (2009). *Indian slavery in colonial America*. U of Nebraska Press.

34. Garfinkel, I. (1988). "The evolution of child support policy". Focus, 11(1), 11-16.

35. Gary, K. (2004). *Social choice and southern secession in the United States*. Homo Oeconomicus, 21, 355-72.

36. Gaspar, D. B., & Hine, D. C. (Eds.). (1996). *More than*

chattel: Black women and slavery in the Americas. Indiana University Press.

37. Geggus, D. P. (2012). *Saint-Domingue on the eve of the Haitian Revolution. In Haitian history* (pp. 82-98). Routledge.

38. Great Rivers Greenway (n.d.). "Who is Mary Meachum"? Missouri Division of Tourism. Retrieved April 17, 2023, from https://greatriversgreenway.org/mary-meachum/

39. Greenwood, J. T. (2010). *First Fruits of Freedom: The Migration of Former Slaves and Their Search for Equality in Worcester, Massachusetts, 1862-1900.* Univ of North Carolina Press.

40. Harper, C. W. (1978). "House servants and field hands: Fragmentation in the antebellum slave community". The North Carolina Historical Review, 55(1), 42-59.

41. Hall, R. E. (Ed.). (2012). *The melanin millennium: Skin color as 21st century international discourse.* Springer Science & Business Media.

42. Harvey, R. D., Tennial, R. E., & Hudson Banks, K. (2017). "The development and validation of a colorism scale". Journal of Black Psychology, 43(7), 740-764.

43. Heck, F. H. (1955). "John C. Breckinridge in the Crisis of 1860-1861". The Journal of Southern History, 21(3), 316-346.

44. Higgins, W. R. (1976). "Charleston: Terminus and entrepôt of the colonial slave trade. In The African Diaspora: Interpretive Essays" (pp. 114-131). Harvard University Press.

45. Hollis, D. W. (1984). *David L. Carlton. Mill and Town in South Carolina, 1880–1920.* Baton Rouge: Louisiana State University Press. 1982. Pp. xii, 313.

46. Jacobs, H. A. (2022). *Incidents in the Life of a Slave Girl.*

47. Jacobs, H., & Jones, B. (2019). *Legacies of Music, Slave Narratives and Autobiography.* Neglected American

Women Writers of the Long Nineteenth Century.

48. Jensen, E. M. (2014). *Three-Fifths Clause--Article I, Section 2, Clause 3. The Heritage Guide to the Constitution, Fully Revised 2nd ed.* (Washington, DC: The Heritage Foundation and Regnery Publishing, 2014), 67-68.

49. Keefer, K. H. (2019). *Marked by fire: brands, slavery, and identity. Slavery & Abolition*, 40(4), 659-681.

50. Keene, J. D. (2002). "A comparative study of white and black American soldiers during the First world war". In Annales de démographie historique (No. 1, pp. 71-90). Cairn/Softwin.

51. Keith, V. M. & Herring, C. (1991). "Skin tone and stratification in the Black community". American Journal of Sociology, 97 (3), 760-778.

52. Kerr, A. E. (2005). "The paper bag principle: Of the myth and the motion of colorism". Journal of American Folklore, 118(469), 271-289.

53. Kersten, A. E. (2000). *Race, Jobs, and the War: the FEPC in the Midwest, 1941-46*. University of Illinois Press.

54. Kersten, A. E. (2002). *African Americans and World War II*. OAH Magazine of History, 16(3), 13-17.

55. Kornweibel Jr, T. (2002). *Investigate Everything": Federal Efforts to Ensure Black Loyalty during World War I*. Indiana University Press.

56. Lennon, C. (2016). "Slave escape, prices, and the fugitive slave act of 1850". The Journal of Law and Economics, 59(3), 669-695.

57. Lewis, K. E. (1985). *Plantation layout and function in the South Carolina Lowcountry*. The Archaeology of Slavery and Plantation Life, 35-65.

58. Lincoln, A. (2015). "Emancipation Proclamation, January 1, 1863". National Archives, 6.

59. Martin, B. L. (1991). "From Negro to Black to African

American: The power of names and naming". Political Science Quarterly, 106(1), 83-107.

60. Maloney, T. N. (1994). "Wage compression and wage inequality between black and white males in the United States, 1940–1960". The Journal of Economic History, 54(2), 358-381.

61. McInnis, M. D. (2005). *The politics of taste in antebellum Charleston.* UNC Press Books.

62. McInnis, M. D. (2011). *Slaves Waiting for Sale: Abolitionist Art and the American Slave Trade.* University of Chicago Press.

63. McKittrick, K. (2006). *Demonic grounds: Black women and the cartographies of struggle.* U of Minnesota Press.

64. Menard, R. R. (1994). "Financing the low country export boom: Capital and growth in early South Carolina". The William and Mary Quarterly, 51(4), 659-676.

65. Monaghan, E. J. (1998). "Reading for the enslaved, writing for the free: Reflections on liberty and literacy". In Proceedings of the American Antiquarian Society (Vol. 108, No. 2, p. 309). American Antiquarian Society.

66. Mungo, T. (2009). "What were some of the responses of the black community in South Carolina during the period of reconstruction to the many challenges they encountered in securing their civil rights".

67. Neville, C. E. (1927). "Origin and Development of the Public High School in Philadelphia". The School Review, 35(5), 363-375.

68. Newman, M. (2002). The Dixiecrat Revolt and the End of the Solid South, 1932-1968. Journal of American Studies, 36, 520.

69. Nicholas, T., & Scherbina, A. (2013). "Real estate prices during the roaring twenties and the great depression". Real Estate Economics, 41(2), 278-309.

70. Nolen, R. M. (2003). *Hoecakes, hambone, and all that jazz: African American traditions in Missouri (Vol. 1).*

University of Missouri Press.

71. Odum, H. W. (1913). "Negro children in the public schools of Philadelphia". The Annals of the American Academy of Political and Social Science, 49(1), 186-208.

72. Ollie Jr, B. W. (1988). "School desegregation efforts in the city of brotherly love". Equity & Excellence, 24(2), 48-52.

73. Olwell, R. (1998). "Masters, slaves, & subjects: The culture of power in the South Carolina Low Country", 1740-1790. Cornell University Press.

74. O'reilly, K. (1997). "The Jim Crow Policies of Woodrow Wilson". The Journal of Blacks in Higher Education, (17), 117-121.

75. Paton, D. (2001). "Punishment, crime, and the bodies of slaves in eighteenth-century Jamaica". Journal of Social History, 923-954.

76. Pusey, A. (2016). "The 14th Amendment Is Ratified". ABAJ, 102, 72.

77. Mandle, J. R. (1992). *Not slave, not free: The African American economic experience since the Civil War.* Duke University Press.

78. Reed, J. S. (1988). "Southern folk, plain and fancy: Native white social types (Vol. 29)". University of Georgia Press.

79. Reichel, P. L. (1988). "Southern slave patrols as a transitional police type". Am. J. Police, 7, 51.

80. Renka, C. E. (2002). "Escaping the auction block and rejecting the pedestal of virtue: slave narratives redefine womanhood in nineteenth-century America".

81. Roberts, F. (2014). *The American foreign legion: black soldiers of the 93d in World War I.* Naval Institute Press.

82. Russell, K., Wilson, M., & Hall, R. E. (1993). The color complex: The politics of skin color among African Americans. Anchor.

83. Schwartz, M. J. (2009). *Born in bondage: Growing up enslaved in the antebellum South.* Harvard University Press.

84. Shlomowitz, R. (1979). "The origins of Southern sharecropping. Agricultural History", 53(3), 557-575.

85. Seidman, J. (1946). *Negro Labor: A National Problem.*

86. Silva, C. (2009). *Racial Restrictive Covenants History. Seattle Civil Rights & Labor History Project.*

87. Singer, A. (2012). "We may never know the real Harriet Tubman". Afro-Americans in New York Life and History, 36(1), 64.

88. Smith, T. W. (1992). Changing racial labels: From "colored" to "negro" to "Black" to "African American". Public Opinion Quarterly, 56(4), 496-514.

89. Smithers, G. D. (2012). *Slave breeding: sex, violence, and memory in African American History.*

90. Smithers, G. D. (2012). "American abolitionism and slave-breeding discourse: a re-evaluation. Slavery & Abolition", 33(4), 551-570.

91. Snodgrass, M. E. (2015). *Civil disobedience: An encyclopedic history of dissidence in the United States. Routledge.*

92. Spencer, J. M. (1992). Black hymnody: a hymnological history of the African-American church. Univ. of Tennessee Press.

93. Stromberg, J. (1979). *The war for southern independence: A radical libertarian perspective.* Journal of Libertarian Studies, 3(1), 31-54.

94. Tabak, R. P. (1990). *The transformation of Jewish identity: the Philadelphia experience, 1919-1945.* Temple University.

95. Thorndale, W., & Dollarhide, W. (1987). *Map guide to the US federal censuses, 1790-1920.* Genealogical Publishing Com.

96. Tindall, G. B. (2021). *South Carolina Negroes, 1877-*

1900. Univ. of South Carolina Press.

97. VanDeburg, W. L. (1978). "Who were the slave drivers"? Negro History Bulletin, 41(2), 808.

98. Wagner, H. L., & Fish, B. D. (2007). *The History of the Democratic Party*. Infobase Publishing.

99. West, E. (2004). *Chains of love: Slave couples in antebellum South Carolina*. University of Illinois Press.

100. Williams, T. H. (1946). "An Analysis of Some Reconstruction Attitudes". The Journal of Southern History, 12(4), 469-486.

101. Woods, L. L. (2012). "The Federal Home Loan Bank Board, redlining, and the national proliferation of racial lending discrimination, 1921–1950". Journal of Urban History, 38(6), 1036-1059.

102. Zierden, M. (1999). "A trans-Atlantic merchant's house in Charleston: Archaeological exploration of refinement and subsistence in an urban setting". Historical Archaeology, 33, 73-87.

A Note About the Author

Arthur D. Vaughn is an educator, scholar, writer, and public intellectual. He received his undergraduate degree from Syracuse University, master's degrees from Clark Atlanta University and Kennesaw State University, and his Ed.D from the University of Georgia. He lives in Marietta, Georgia.